MY BERLIN CHILD

Anne Wiazemsky

MY BERLIN CHILD

*Translated from the French
by Alison Anderson*

Europa
editions

Europa Editions
116 East 16th Street
New York, N.Y. 10003
www.europaeditions.com
info@europaeditions.com

Translation by Alison Anderson
Original Title: *Mon enfant de Berlin*
Translation copyright © 2010 by Europa Editions

Library of Congress Cataloging in Publication Data is available
ISBN 978-1-60945-003-8

Wiazemsky, Anne
My Berlin Child

Book design by Emanuele Ragnisco
www.mekkanografici.com
Cover photo © Popperfoto/Getty Images

Prepress by Grafica Punto Print – Rome

Printed in Canada

To the memory of Claire,
Wia, and their friends at
96 Kurfürstendamm.

MY BERLIN CHILD

Claire is an ambulance driver with the French Red Cross. It is September, 1944, and she is still in Béziers with her section: she is twenty-seven years old, a very pretty young woman with large dark eyes and high Slavic cheekbones. Whenever she receives compliments, she pretends to ignore them. She has no time to look at herself in the mirror, or when she does, it is only fleetingly, and always mistrustfully. Since she joined the Red Cross a year and a half ago, she has been striving to make her work her whole existence. Her superiors greatly admire her mental and physical courage and her enthusiasm. Her fellow workers, often from social backgrounds that are very different from her own, have forgotten that she is the daughter of a famous writer, François Mauriac, and they look on her as one of them, nothing more. This makes her happy. She loves what she is doing, the need to live one day at a time. When she is behind the wheel of her ambulance, rushing wounded men to overcrowded hospitals, she feels alive for the first time in her young life. Hers is a life without a past, without a future; a life in the present.

From her room she looks out over the roofs of Béziers. A golden late afternoon light illuminates the tiles. Bells are ringing. On the big table that serves as a desk are her precious wireless and a bouquet of garden roses. Next to the vase is a notebook, and when she has time she writes down the narrative of her days: her diary. There are numerous photographs of her parents, her brothers, and her sister with her baby. Another photograph, off to one side, portrays a young man in uniform with a forced smile on his face. There are times she looks at him with tenderness, lovingly, but lately, more and more, she avoids him.

Just now she is attentive only to her feelings—a physical well-being provoked by the soft air and a copious meal of tomatoes, eggs, and prunes they found in an abandoned farm. Soon there will be more meals, and she will no longer be hungry. Even though there is still fighting, isn't the war nearly over?

Which raises another question: will she have to go back to her family, as they have requested, or will she disobey and follow the army? Most of her companions have already made their choice one way or the other.

Claire lights a cigarette. To breathe in the smoke and then exhale through her nostrils is a pleasure she never tires of. Even in the worst moments, smoking a cigarette, any cigarette, helps her to face her daily concerns and find the necessary self-detachment. A young lieutenant she just met has given her an entire carton he got from the American army. In exchange, she is supposed to show him around the countryside. But they haven't set a date, and as a soldier he might be called back to combat any day now.

She looks out again through her window onto the rooftops of Béziers. She has loved this town from the very first, and the knowledge she will soon be leaving fills her with genuine sorrow. Where will she be going? There it is again, the question she does not know how to answer.

She picks up her notebook, stretches out on the bed, and begins to leaf through it as if going over her past might help her to decide her future. She skims through the pages devoted to her early days in Caen, then lingers over the ones where she talks about Patrice, who is a prisoner in Germany: they've been corresponding since the beginning of the war. "My fiancé," she says softly, "my fiancé . . . " She looks up at his portrait by the flower vase and considers it carefully. It seems to her that she no longer quite remembers the way he moves or the timbre of his voice.

On December 19, 1943, during a brief stay in Paris, she wrote:

> Spent the whole day with Patrice's parents, although I only came for lunch. It's extraordinary how I love his family. I truly feel like I'm one of them. His brothers resemble him a great deal. Naturally we spoke about Patrice. How they love him and how that love extends to me. In their eyes I am the woman Patrice loves, and can do no wrong. Not to mention the fact they think I'm very pretty.
>
> I've changed so much since last year! A year ago I was so very unhappy. Patrice meant nothing, or almost nothing, to me, whereas now he is becoming more and more important to me with each passing day. It used to bore me just to think of him, and I was dreading his return. But now I am counting the days—I want to see him, touch him, speak to him, thank him for loving me so much, for showing me how to love him, how to wait for him with so much joy and impatience.
>
> A year ago I failed the entrance exam to the Red Cross. I was upset, I had no faith in myself. Today I know that I am a capable person. It's the end of the year and I am pleased with how far I have come. I think that Caen has really been good for me. I am less selfish—and above all I know better how to appreciate true happiness. I am not as blasé, and I love myself less for myself than for Patrice. I am waiting for him. Simply imagining our apartment and my life at his side brings me pleasure.

On the pages that follow, Claire has painstakingly copied out every letter she has sent to Patrice. She narrates fragments of her everyday life, but more than anything she enjoys dreaming about their future in a world at peace. She is sentimental, and this, along with the constant repetition of how much she loves him, suddenly exasperates her. "What childish nonsense!" she thinks. And immediately afterwards: "I really have committed myself!" She forgets that her letters are in response to Patrice's, which she has stored in her suitcase and rarely rereads. "There isn't time," she says out loud, as if someone had asked her why; she hasn't written to him for several days now, and a touch of remorse spoils her last puffs on her cigarette. She hurries over the pages that irritate her, lighting a new cigarette from the last one. Better to go back to more flattering episodes: these are surely a truer reflection of the young woman she has become, she thinks, thanks to the war. As is often the case, this is a letter she copied out before giving it to a companion on leave to pass on. It is addressed to her family at 38 Avenue Théophile-Gautier, Paris, 16th arrondissement.

August 21, 1944

My dear darling parents, I've just begun to realize that I am in a free country and I can write whatever I want. I think about you all the time. Night before last, when every wireless was blasting the news of the liberation of Paris, I was so sorry not to be there that I could have wept. At that moment I would have given everything I've experienced over these last few months with the FRC to have been for those few hours in Paris.

I expect you'll have seen some extraordinary things, and I'm almost ashamed to tell you how little I've been doing.

German convoys went through Béziers for days on end. But we continued our missions along the overcrowded roads. I would sit on the fender of the car and gaze up at the sky, wondering . . . Several times we got trapped in the most enormous convoys. It was impossible to get out, except when the planes were above us, because then the column would stop by the side of the road. There was often Allied machine-gun fire, but never directly above us. We could tell what was happening from the expression on the Germans' faces, and from their burning vehicles.

Last Sunday, the town was strafed. From five to nine o'clock in the evening, the tanks rolled through the streets with their machine guns firing: fifteen dead, fifty wounded. Imagine your little Claire with her friend Martine and an agent, taking half an hour just to get to my ambulance. The most dangerous thing was crossing the major avenues. You'd take a step then have to hug the wall because of the spray of bullets. Finally we ended up walking slowly down the middle of the street showing our badges and raising our arms. Several times they aimed their guns at us then lowered them. We spent over four hours going through the streets of Béziers, collecting the wounded. Bullets whistling everywhere, it was incredible. The Germans never aimed right at us. At one point I was between two tanks and a German soldier motioned to me to put on a helmet. I wasn't afraid, and if it weren't for the dead and wounded, I would have been mad with joy. There's a man who would have bled to death if it hadn't been for Martine and me. He knows it, and every time we go to the hospital he thanks us. You've no idea how good that makes me feel—and it makes up for so much else.

I spent the next two days going from morgue to morgue. I saw horrible wounds; there was one very young girl, dead, and her mother wouldn't let go of her. A young Résistance fighter—his mouth full of worms, etc. etc. I went to get ten coffins.

Then the men from the Résistance arrived. They weren't very handsome, or very enthusiastic. For an entire day they went around shooting from the roofs and the streets at more or less imaginary *miliciens*. In the meantime I was transporting people who'd been wounded in a minor aerial bombardment. The planes flew overhead, strafing everywhere. I didn't even have time to realize that I too might die.

Yesterday we answered an urgent call to go and fetch some wounded men from the Maquis at Saint-Pons. I personally was thrilled to hear that they were still fighting. But when we got there, all we found was complete calm after several days of fighting. The Germans had thoroughly pillaged the town and were going to burn everything when they noticed they had thirty or more wounded men. We began to administer first aid, they saw they were going to be well treated, and they said, "We will do our duty as you are doing yours." And they left. The wounded men from the Maquis had already been evacuated, so we took the Germans who were badly wounded back to Béziers. I stayed with them at the hospital for an hour. They were in such pain that it made me sick. I would have liked to hate them, but all I felt was immense pity; if only there were some way to relieve their suffering. One of them, a poor boy of only eighteen, had peritonitis. He was done for, and the doctor didn't want to operate on him. His hand clung to mine, burning, and his eyes were so full of plead-

ing that I began to cry. I thought about all the men like him who
are dying, far from their families. I'm not cut out to be a nurse, I
would be too unhappy.

Five o'clock in the afternoon. I've just been to fetch a man who
died before my eyes as a result of Sunday's strafing. I don't like seeing dead bodies but what's even worse is the families, the sobbing.
The air is heavy, the town is full of members of the Résistance,
stars, and flags. We hope to see the Americans soon in the port of
Sète. Would you believe that the landings were supposed to be
there, at Sète, Agde, etc. They only asked for maps of the Riviera
ten days before the landings.

Claire closes her notebook in order to think about what she
has just read and clear her mind. She quickly concludes that she
has a certain courage in action and, what's more, a taste for it.
"A healthy dose of recklessness, more like!" her section leader
would lecture. Claire, in the quiet of her room, would reply,
natural as can be, "I like danger."

She stubs out her cigarette, stands up, and goes to lean her
elbows on the windowsill. The sun is setting, casting shadows
over the roofs. In the sky, swallows trace ever smaller circles
and sing loudly, as if to greet the end of the day and the onset
of night. Down in the courtyard, two of her comrades are on
their way out for dinner in town. Like Claire, their day off is
nearly over and they have swapped their "RAF blue" uniforms for outfits that make them look like any other women.
Claire is tempted to join them, but she doesn't really feel like
it, or at least not yet. There will be time, soon enough, to do
the rounds of the two or three cafés where they are regulars.
There is something both delightful and strange about this day
during which there has not been a single alert; a silence over
the town. It's almost as if she missed her dear ambulance. She
doesn't know what the coming week has in store—which
brings her back to the decision she'll have to make a few days
from now.

Nightfall brings a new chill to the air: Claire shivers. She puts a sweater on over her blouse, lights the lamps, and looks with satisfaction at her reflection in the large mirror above the fireplace. Her suntanned face looks rested, her features relaxed. Gone is the grave expression she so frequently wears and which those who are close to her find so unsettling. She fluffs out her thick brown hair, which she washed that very morning, and notices that she has neglected her hands: they are like a working girl's. Where is she supposed to find nail polish or manicure tools? In Paris she'd be able to have whatever she wanted—the cozy comfort of her parents' apartment, as much food as she liked, and a fire to keep warm, what with winter on the way. Like everyone in France, she has suffered terribly from the cold during the years of war. What she really likes about Béziers is the climate—sunny days, a relentless blue sky. Suddenly her reflection in the mirror loses its charm, is replaced by fear, a desperation she had almost forgotten but which had never really left her. She turns away from the mirror and switches on the wireless: the first movement of Mozart's Clarinet Concerto, the allegro. During the darkest hours of the Occupation her father would find sustenance in listening to Mozart. Sometimes he would shut himself away in the drawing room, all alone, to be right in the heart of the music. And he would say that in the andante there was "something like a reproach to God, the complaint of a disappointed child." She breathes more easily already. Perhaps she ought to settle comfortably in bed to read, with her notebook in one hand and a fresh cigarette in the other. This is the continuation of the letter to her parents that she copied out and where for the first time she told them everything about her life in Béziers that she had kept secret.

August 28, 1944
Yesterday there was a major political demonstration. I thought

about Paris and everything seemed terribly ugly and small. And yet there was a fine ceremony by the wall where I had gone to get the corpses of eight people executed by firing squad. Life here is so calm you could cry. I have no intention of hanging about. I've had no news from you for too long, not a word from Papa. Perhaps I'll have the joy of hearing his voice on the wireless before long.

I remember how I wrote to you, really miserable letters, practically farewells, I was so afraid of dying. My fear came not only from the corpses I saw, or the bombing, but above all from the life we've been leading up to now. Just think, from January until now our section was where all the Résistance leaders in the region would meet. Until the landings, two or three of them would come every day for lunch and they often stayed overnight at the section. Our leader was a liaison agent; the house was full of weapons, and I can't count how many arms, explosives, Maquis leaders, etc., my ambulance transported. We went to pick up the wounded maquisards; we would warn the Maquis of German raids. I confess it wasn't exactly relaxing, and there were times I was afraid, such as when we were waiting for Renée and she only came back several hours after the scheduled time. We spent an entire night waiting for her! And the Résistance leader said, "If she's not here by midnight, I'll have to run for it, because the Gestapo cannot be far behind." So he left, and we went on waiting. One night I went up on the roof with one of them to hide all our revolvers under the tiles. I remember there was such a beautiful moon, and the oddest things went through my mind.

That day when I had to pick up the bodies from the firing squad, I didn't want to go because I was so afraid I might know one of them. And when I saw the body of this poor woman who hadn't done a thing, I thought about myself and had a terrible urge to throw up. Not a terribly elegant way to react, but there was nothing for it; I could see myself in a pool of blood as if my death had already happened.

I would have liked to keep a journal but it was out of the question, far too dangerous. The Gestapo was looking for a woman by the name of Renée, but they never got as far as us. We were always on the alert, and I had a passport ready for Spain. There were times I took a revolver with me when I went on a mission, and I assure you, I would have known how to use it. Fortunately we were on very good terms with the Kommandantur, who gave us the permits we asked for, because we had done good work during the bombing. Moreover, they really trusted the French Red Cross. I found this side of the whole business really unpleasant, because if we had been caught it would have compromised the FRC, which is a first-rate, remarkable organization. Ours were the only vehicles they almost never stopped. That is what we gambled on, and nearly every time we made it through. On the rare instances when they stopped the ambulance, they would find a maquisard playing the wounded man, so they quickly closed the door without asking for any papers and said, "Much work, very good!"

I don't know if you got the letter where I tried to make you understand that I had gone to see the Maquis. I left one morning with two section doctors and the leader of the *Francs-tireurs partisans* to go to their Maquis high in the mountains.

For forty-eight hours I went all around the Maquis, helping to hand out medicine, treating people, and bringing back the sick and wounded. At the end of the first day, I had just filled the tank on the ambulance with the help of a *Résistant* when we went past a huge supply truck. He made me drive right alongside him, and with his machine gun aimed at the driver of the truck he ordered him to follow us. That night we had a regular feast in the Maquis! I can't even begin to tell you about the dinner, the evening we spent around the campfire, the singing. Or about our return in the middle of the night with our headlights hardly working, and your little Claire who stopped just in time at the edge of a precipice, or about the night in the ambulance lying on blood-stained stretchers, with dirty blankets that had covered I don't know how many sick or dead people, or about the sleep that finally came. The next morning, we set off again at seven o'clock.

I've suddenly thought about the landings, and I have to tell you that we recognized all the messages. So you can imagine how excited we were when the first ones came through. What we didn't realize was that some of the messages, like, "To my command, attention!" or, *"Il en rougit, le traître!"* were for all of France! So on the day before the first landing, when we heard them, we thought they were for us! What a night! Everyone was there. One of the men, who is now a captain, was preparing all the explosives in the drawing room, and an hour later he carried out THE GREEN PLAN, which meant blowing everything up. We girls could hear it, and with each new explosion we said, He hasn't been taken yet. It was so disappointing not to hear anything more, and to find out the next day that they had landed at Caen.

> Bravant le froid,
> Bravant la faim,
> Bravant les chiens,
> Sans jamais perdre courage,
> Ce sont ceux du Maquis,
> Ceux de la Résistance,
> Ce sont ceux du Maquis,
> Jeunesse du pays . . . [1]

Claire hums the tune she heard in the maquis during the wonderful improvised dinner around the campfire. She's not sure about the words, or the music, but the song makes her shiver with emotion and pride. She'll have to find someone who can tell her the exact lyrics so that she can copy them out in her diary. She turns to read one last entry.

Saturday, September 2, 1944

Hello my dear darling parents. I haven't heard from you in ages. The only thing that will make me happy is getting a letter telling me that you're all fine. I am doing very well indeed. I'm working a great deal, but the missions are so dull I could cry.

There's nothing new at this end. It's raining—fortunately, because for over a week the heat has been merciless.

Yesterday I was sound asleep when I had to go and fetch two men with gunshot wounds. Imagine a first young man, FFI, naturally: he pulls out his revolver, points at the other agent and says, "I'm sure yours is not as pretty as mine." The agent says, "Steady . . . point your weapon the other way." "Where's the danger?" says the first man, and he removes the cartridge clip, aims at his belly, and fires.

---

[1] Braving the cold / Living with hunger / Braving the dogs / And never losing heart / Our men from the maquis / Our men from the Résistance / Our men from the maquis / The youth of our land...

There was a bullet in the barrel: it went right through him and went to lodge in the liver of a man who was standing behind him. I don't know if it was because I stood up too abruptly, or the sight of all that blood and vomit and their terrible faces, but I was overwhelmed by nausea and had to leave the operating room.

Just this minute I learned that they both died. There have been countless numbers of accidents with weapons. I don't understand why they don't disarm all those kids. They're so proud of themselves that they end up spending all their time playing with their toys.

Above all, don't go telling everyone what we did with our ambulances for the Résistance. Don't forget that we work under the banner of the FRC and we had no right to do what we did. It's about time I started working openly for the Army. I don't have the soul of a spy.

On the wireless, the Clarinet Concerto has come to an end. Claire has heard it often, so she knows this is the third movement, the rondo. She thinks about two of her dearest friends, "wooers" as her family calls them, who are somewhere still fighting the Germans, and she has not had any news from them for a long time. Quite spontaneously, each on his own initiative, they both began calling her "Clarinette." Where are they now? Are they even alive?

Two quick knocks on the door, and it opens. A disheveled blonde head appears in the frame. Eyes the blue of forget-me-nots, an upstart little nose, an irresistible smile: this is Martine, her favorite co-worker, whose constant good cheer has sustained her on more than one occasion.

"I'm going down to the kitchen to make us a bite to eat. Are you coming? After that we'll go and see if the others are at the café."

"I'll be there in five minutes."

She closes the door gently behind her but her cork wedge heels tap loudly along the corridor. Claire puts her notebook to one side, picks up a pen and pad, and begins to write.

Béziers, September 21

My dear parents, if the war truly is over everywhere, I will soon be with you, but if it continues, I'll go up to the front. I hope with all my heart that it will be over soon so that I can see you again and all this suffering will come to an end. But if it goes on, I'll go gladly to the front.

She has told them the most important thing, but maybe she has put it too abruptly, maybe she should be a bit more tactful, and consider the shock they'll get when they read her letter. Perhaps she should begin by telling them how she spent her day off? Or ask for their news? It's easy enough, she can rewrite the letter when she comes back from her evening out. For the time being it's as if an enormous burden had been lifted from her shoulders, and she must tell Martine right away, and maybe the other girls, too, what she's decided.

Monday, October 9, 1944, midnight
The day after tomorrow I'll be leaving Béziers. I'm inexpressibly happy, but it also makes me so sad. Another chapter of my life coming to an end. Nine months! An entire lifetime, and what a life! I've been happy here, and I shall miss almost everything. If I weren't leaving to see my family again to go and be with the Army, I think I should cry my heart out. Despite my joy, I am sad, terribly sad. I think that Béziers has been the most beautiful chapter of my life. I have lived life to the fullest here, utterly.

She gazes at a simple metal ring with a fake amethyst, a ring a little girl would wear. The young lieutenant she met in September just gave it to her. Tonight he's the one filling all her thoughts.

I find it so hard to leave him all alone, so alone. His sorrow devastates me and this evening I wasn't even happy anymore at the thought of seeing my parents and yet . . . if I weren't leaving him, I wouldn't be this sad, but I know he's unhappy so I cannot be happy. I shall never forget him. He has been my guardian angel. He truly loved me and I am grateful to him for everything he has given me. I shall never forget his face, his eyes. That's life, there's no point in crying, but I can still remember. How stupid it is to grow so attached. This life has changed me so much. I was just a kid, now I'm a woman.

Claire gets up and puts on her fur coat. In the fireplace the last logs have burned down, and the few remaining embers no longer give off any heat. She blows onto her stiff fingers, and rubs them together. Outside it is pouring. A heavy downpour that has lasted for two days and which makes her forget that she is in the south of France. She feels ill at ease because of what she has just written. Why did she let herself go, writing about this man, when she swore she would never mention his existence? When they met, she told him she was engaged, and would soon be leaving Béziers. She was also putting into practice what the war has taught her: to live for the moment. She never imagined their encounter would bring her anything more than a fleeting sense of well-being; she believed she was strong, well armed against heartache, against what she scornfully referred to as "sorrows of the heart."

To distract herself, Claire looks at family photographs. In one of them her very pregnant sister Luce is on the floor playing with her little girl, who is two. Their two brothers, Claude, the elder one, and Jean, the younger, are on either side of her, smiling at the lens. They are both smoking, with a pseudo-virile attitude. The scene is set in their parents' drawing room on the avenue Théophile-Gautier. Claire supposes they have just had lunch, and are drinking coffee—well, some sort of ersatz coffee. Have they been getting enough to eat? In Béziers, she has not been able to eat her fill, and there are days when food becomes an obsession. Like so many other people in France, she naïvely believed that victory would bring a renewed profusion of supplies. During the war, daily life was so hard, so dangerous, that she had never had the time to think about it too much. Now she returns to her notebook.

Mama wrote to me that the thought of my leaving for the Army fills them with despair. Perhaps it really is my duty to stay with them. And yet I know I will leave. They'll be unhappy and that will hurt. Can one ever be completely happy? Someone always has to suffer.

Claude went by plane to Normandy to fetch some things belonging to De Gaulle. Papa is once again my Papa from before the war. Why do I love my family so much? I am proud of them. Sometimes I'm afraid that fate will take revenge for all the happiness my loved ones bring me and the easy, happy life I have had up to now. So I think of the men who have died, and those who will be shot, and the prisoners.

I won't mention Patrice, the situation doesn't bear thinking about. He is suffering, too. I haven't even done what I could have done for him. The thought of his return, and the way I behaved two years ago, frighten me. I don't want to think about it, there are so many things keeping us apart. Poor Patrice! But then, why hasn't he come back? It's his fault.

I'm tired and freezing. How strange and sad life is.

Tuesday, October 10, midnight
That's it, I won't see him ever again. For the first time in my life I've seen a man cry, he was so terribly miserable. It's very moving and upsetting to see a man cry. I would never have thought it could be so beautiful. This afternoon we went to the beach together. The sea was beautiful and we were sad.

We're leaving tomorrow at 6 A.M.! Farewell, Béziers.

Claire closes her notebook places it in the suitcase already containing all her clothes and the books she never had time to read. Tomorrow she'll be traveling in uniform, with her little gold cross of Lorraine pinned to her lapel. A cross of Lorraine which General de Gaulle gave to each of François Mauriac's four children, and she is very proud of it. Claire wants recognition as a Red Cross ambulance driver, a combatant. On the walls she will leave behind the maps of France, Italy, and Russia that she had pinned up upon her arrival, so that she could follow the Allies' progress. The wireless is broadcasting Vivaldi's Mandolin Concerto. Claire feels her sadness begin to ebb. What she has just written is the truth. His tears made a tremendous impression on her. Were it not for that, she suspects she would have felt greater indifference. She picks up the photographs and puts them into her handbag. The photograph of Patrice puts her in a bad mood. What would he do if she left him? Would he be able to cry, to succumb to his sorrow in her presence, to show his vulnerability? She thinks he would act as he does in every circumstance, with courage and dignity. She almost feels angry at him for enlisting before call-up and spending the entire war as a prisoner in Germany. She suddenly recalls how in the beginning she found him somewhat dull. But then he volunteered to lead a disciplinary battalion and her opinion changed: how brave of him! And just to think that this heroic man had fallen hopelessly in love with her—how could she fail to be delighted, charmed? Her contact with him would make her a better person, he would help her grow up and become someone, not just "the charming little Mauriac girl." And now, after four years of war, she has been moved by this other man's fragility . . . Patrice has no idea that she is no longer the young girl he knew. "I was just a kid, and now I'm a woman," she thinks, over and over. And what about him, what has become of him? In his letters there has not been even a hint of the slightest change.

Suddenly she stops thinking and a gut fear stops her in her tracks. She can feel the migraine coming; she recognizes the warning signs. Migraines, her old enemy . . . they had almost vanished during the summer, then they began again in early September, not too frequent at first, then they began coming closer and closer together. They are often followed by terrible stomach aches that confine her to her bed in the dark for twenty-four hours, or even forty-eight. She knows that the train journey tomorrow will be no easier than during wartime: there will be delays, unexpected stops, and too many people for too few seats. How can she possibly get to Paris if she's nauseous after the migraine, which now seems a certainty?

Claire is unable to take the train the next day. She spends two days in bed, flat on her back with the pain. Her companions take turns bringing her hot tea because it is the only thing she can keep down. They have learned to be silent: the slightest noise is like a drill in her skull. The rest of the time they go back and forth between the prison and the hospital to transfer the ones who are worst off. There is worried talk about an outbreak of typhus.

Only the dog Freddy, the section mascot, is allowed to stay in Claire's room. She lies three feet from the bed with her muzzle on her paws, keeping watch over the girl who found her during the first Allied bombings, when she was famished and covered in sores. Now her moist, loving gaze never leaves Claire: the young woman is moaning unrestrainedly.

A car is being sent to bring medicine and surgical material back from Paris, and they have agreed to drive Claire to her parents' house. Still very weak, she leaves all the driving to her colleague and stretches out on the back seat to watch the landscape go by. She did not expect to see such devastation, so many ruins, rutted, torn up roads, and virtually everywhere the traces of bombardment and fires. Every face she glimpses is marked with fear and hunger. The rain and the low, dark sky accentuate the desolation of the countryside. "My poor France," murmurs Claire, with a heavy heart. In the front seat her companion is silent, concentrating on her driving, difficult as it is. She will manage, she's used to it. But Claire supposes that both of them must be feeling the same despondency.

Gradually they leave Béziers behind, and the Paris she was so eager to see again begins to lose some of its attraction. What will she do back among her family? What purpose will she serve? She can hardly picture herself going back to typing and shorthand classes, like the ones she was taking before she joined the Red Cross. The head office has not yet replied to her request to be transferred to the Army in eastern France, where the war is still being fought. It's not that she thinks they might refuse, no, the Red Cross needs staff. She just hopes that it will be decided quickly, and that she won't have time to be sucked into family routine, into all the comfort and distractions of Paris. Her friend Martine agrees with her. She has been reunited with her fiancé, who was wounded during the liberation of the capital. Now she is looking after him at her future in-laws' house, but as soon as possible he will rejoin his battalion. Martine wants to be on an equal footing with him, wants to run the same risks, share the same hardship, and fight for a free world. Claire envies the way her friend always knows how to run her life, finding it so easy to tell the good choices from the bad; she envies her for still loving the first boy who ever kissed her.

She looks indifferently at the little girl's ring on her finger, then pulls it off and slips it into her jacket pocket. During the excruciating stomach pains that kept her in her room, she forgot all about the young man who had wept before her. He belonged to the Béziers episode in her life, and that episode has come to an end. Lying in the back of the car, she has no idea what the next episode will be. Her desire to join the Army is all tangled up with her dread of Patrice's return. She does not want to wait for him, she wants to get out of Paris before he comes to find her, with his love and his marriage proposal. She needs more time, to be sure of her feelings.

By the time the car reaches Paris, after a few detours, the rain has stopped. Night fell long ago, and there is not much light behind the closed shutters, nor have all the street lamps been lit. There are still a few cars along the deserted streets. When they reach the Place de la Concorde, the two girls shout for joy at the same time: this is the first time they have seen the Place without the German road signs in Gothic letters. To be sure, there had been photographs in the news stories in the papers, and people had told them, so they knew, but it didn't seem real. Claire sits up straight on the back seat. When they come to a red light, she squeezes her colleague's shoulders. Martine turns around, her face a mixture of extreme fatigue and triumph. As if a signal had passed

between them, they begin to chant at the top of their lungs
the song of the partisans.

Ami, entends-tu le vol noir des corbeaux sur nos plaines,
Ami, entends-tu les cris sourds d'un pays qu'on enchaîne.[2]

[2] Friend, can you hear the crows darkly flying o'er the plains,
Friend, can you hear the deaf cries of a country in chains?

Sunday, October 22, 1944

I've been back in Paris for eleven days already! I confess I haven't felt happy here yet. There has been no joy. None at all.

The other day I heard about Jock's death. This has made me desperately sad. I knew I mightn't see him again, but I kept hoping all the same. He was killed in Italy, in the Cassino region, I think. He was in a jeep: beheaded. Poor Jock, it seems everyone adored him. The others spoke calmly about his death, and no one realized the effect it was having on me. Now I know for sure: I'll never see him at the front, or meet him in the street, or get a letter from him, and I am still just as sad as on the first day. Jock is the only person I've ever loved. The other evening, when I was at the Lido, I felt like crying. All those people dancing made me feel sick. I saw Jock in his coffin. I could picture him, just the way I have seen so many others; it was horrible. It's true, I almost started crying.

Since returning to Paris, I've seen a lot of old friends, but all I felt like saying to any of them was, "It's not you I want to see, it's Jock."

I never think about my lover in Béziers anymore. I've always known I didn't love him.

Farewell, Jock.

Claire hears her name echoing around the apartment, amid exclamations and laughter: her sister Luce has given birth to a second little girl, and has come to show the baby to their parents. Claire does not feel like rushing in to see them. Of course she will go, she must, but in a while. Since her return she has been finding it difficult to fit in with her family and her friends; some of them are still missing. Everyone is very busy so they're not terribly interested in her experiences with the Red Cross. Particularly her father and brothers. Even her minor role in the Résistance has failed to arouse the admiration she so hoped for and needs so badly. Doesn't it simply boil down to the fact that their life, as men, will always be more important? From the start they all tried to convince her that her place, her true place as a woman, was there with her parents. And she resisted: since then, they've stopped talking about it. Now Claire is waiting for her marching orders. She already knows that in the space of a few weeks, perhaps even a few days, she will be leaving with Martine at the wheel of an ambulance for Belfort, where there is still fighting. She is ready, she's had her uniform cleaned and it's waiting, like new, in her wardrobe, with the cross of Lorraine pinned to the lapel.

All it takes to feel alive is to picture herself on the road once again, in the fog and cold and dark. Then the pain, sharp and piercing: she will never see Jock again. She had met him during her vacation in Montgenèvre, near Briançon, where he was doing his military service in 1938. He is the one who got into the habit of calling her Clarinette. André, the other one who calls her by that name, is alive, fighting on the Eastern front. She hopes with all her heart that she will see him again, so she can tell him how afraid she has been; so she can hold him in her arms and tell him how sorry she is: she had not realized he was a hero, a real hero.

She will never forget that day in October, 1943, when she was waiting for him at the Gare de Lyon. He stepped down from the train. She ran up to meet him but a silent "no" in his gaze stopped her in her tracks. A second later, four men from the Gestapo surrounded him, handcuffed him, and brutally shoved him forward. He put up no resistance and obstinately kept his eyes down when they walked past her. Claire had been stunned to begin with, and wanted to go up to him, but a stranger's hand grabbed her by the elbow. A voice murmured in her neck, "Don't do anything, go away . . . You are putting his life in danger . . . " She didn't have time to see the stranger's face because he immediately vanished into the crush of passengers; all she had seen was the tall silhouette of someone who seemed to be a very young man.

Claire left the train station and took the métro, her face a blank slate. Any other expression was impossible; she was in a state of shock. It was only once she got home that she burst into tears. Her father, alarmed, called her up to his study and explained something that she had never known: her friend André had been a member of the Résistance from the very beginning, and the Gestapo had nearly caught him several times already. No doubt now he would be tortured, but her father knew André was a brave man, and he was sure he could keep silent. Then he murmured, "But at such a price, dear God . . . " In a more normal voice he said, "By signaling to you, he saved your life: they would have tortured you to death to make him talk and, undoubtedly, he would have . . . don't ever forget him." In May, 1944, André managed to escape and join a Résistance cell. When Paris was liberated, he had been there.

Her thoughts of Jock and André lead her to two other friends, Michel and Minko. She has heard from them, they are on the Eastern front, alive. But for how long?

Wrapped in her fur coat and hat, with a long woolen scarf around her neck, Claire braves the icy winds of the Esplanade des Invalides. She is passing through Paris after a week spent on the Eastern front, in Belfort, and has just left Patrice's parents' apartment. It was exactly like a year ago, when they greeted her so affectionately that she could not bring herself to leave. She appreciates their simplicity, their patriotism, their love for their three sons. The youngest, Laurent, was there. To them, Claire is Patrice's fiancée and they look on her as a daughter—a daughter they have long desired, because they have only boys. They respect and uphold her commitment to the Red Cross. They understand that she has hardly had time to write to them. But with great discretion, as they talk of other things, they imply that Patrice is concerned, so seldom does she write.

He is still a prisoner in Germany. He has grown very weak, and knows nothing of the movements of the Allied armies. He is suffering more than ever from the cold and hunger, and from a painful feeling of abandonment. In his last message, dating from October, Patrice wrote that he might be transferred to another camp he knows nothing about. Claire was moved by this detail. She is sorry she has thought so little about him, as if she had forgotten him; as if, when she was away from Paris, he became a mere interlude in her life. Now suddenly, in this apartment where he lived before the war together with his parents—they are so like him—Patrice has once again become a real human being.

Claire crosses the Pont Alexandre-III and for a moment she stops to lean against the railing. A real human being: once again she sees so many qualities in him that she thinks she loves him. She wants to help him. Write to him, at least, tell him what she is doing. But where should she write, if he changes camps? The prisoners' conditions must be terrible: the Germans know that they have lost the war. What will be the fate of their prisoners? Will they let them go alive? Will they be liberated? When? For the first time, it occurs to Claire that she would like to follow the armies into the heart of Germany, all the way to Berlin.

Around her the wind has dropped, but a damp fog blurs the landscape. She does not see so much as sense the Place de la Concorde, the Louvre. Paris seems dreary and hostile to her, a reflection of the troubled waters of the Seine. It is a city that is sleeping, petrified, and she is eager to leave. Passersby are few and far between, and they walk quickly, their heads sunk between their shoulders. If she goes back to Belfort, that will show her solidarity with Patrice—that is what she must write to him.

In spite of her warm clothing, her mittens and fur-lined boots, a damp chill is creeping into her bones. She decides to go home, to Avenue Théophile-Gautier.

At the place where the bridge meets the quai she sees a woman holding a little boy by the hand. He is so tangled up in scarves that she cannot see his face. But she hears his voice as she walks by: "Mama, Mama, that lady . . . " Claire freezes, fearful of what he might say next, how he will judge her: " . . . that lady, look how beautiful she is!"

Thursday, December 7, Paris

What I have written about the front is of no interest. When I think back on it, I see something else altogether. When you write every day, you leave out the important things, because they're so obvious; but now, when I think back, I see mud, an endless succession of convoys, Jeep after Jeep, soldiers tramping through the mud, fires at night where the men gathered to get warm. Bridges, rebuilt, where no one ever drives slowly enough, men who are incredibly friendly and always ready with a smile, ready to speak to you, and occasionally they drive past you. And amidst all the mud, a wet snow falling in gusts, a fine day, cold but luminous. Then more ruins, not razed to the ground like after a bombardment, just houses where they've been fighting, with traces of bullets and shells. And now I can see how sweet a warm toasty room would be, and how the cold would pinch you when you went outside again . . .

I'm in a hurry to go back there. My homecoming wasn't pleasant at all . . .

Claire puts down her pen, closes her notebook and takes her head in her hands in a childish gesture of despair. She was trying to set down in writing the week she just spent in Belfort, a terribly important week. She can't do it. The words escape her, and the humiliation of being the worst pupil in the class overwhelms her even now. She can hear the teacher's comments: "You are the daughter of François Mauriac, and just look at all these spelling and grammar mistakes you've made . . . aren't you ashamed?" She remembers how the terrible migraines suddenly came over her and paralyzed her, and made her seem like a complete idiot in the presence of adults or the other pupils in her class. Her parents stubbornly refused to admit that she really was in pain. If at least she had had a fever they would have taken her seriously. But migraines never come with a fever or any other visible symptoms. The upset stomachs came afterwards, entire days in bed; finally they decided to have her stop her studies. She was informed that she was in no state to take her baccalaureate exams, and it would be better to spare her any further failure. As if it were only yesterday, Claire recalls her relief, and the shame that quickly followed.

From the neighboring apartment come the strains of a Chopin sonata, very badly played. Claire does not know the family who live on the other side of the wall of her room, but she has never heard them play a single piece of music properly. As if generations of children in succession were there merely to destroy the poor piano and leave her with a loathing for music.

In actual fact, Claire cannot stand being back in the family apartment. Everything irritates and upsets her, and the slightest thing revives bad memories of childhood and adolescence. The war has taken a strange turn and no one believes anymore in a certain or imminent victory. This too fills her with anguish: she is not in the only place where she is truly needed.

The little clock on her night table tells her that it will soon be time for dinner. She has a sudden urge to have a tête-à-tête with her father, to feel his physical presence. If she dared, she would go and knock on the door of his study. He must be working on an article for *Le Figaro*, or else he's writing some stage notes for his play, *Les Mal-Aimés*. The first performance will be held in January or February at the Comédie-Française. She doesn't know the actors' names, or how the rehearsals are going. She remembers how angry she was when Jean-Louis Vaudoyer turned the play down a first time in 1941. It would do her good to talk about the theater with her father; it would help to justify her enforced presence in Paris. But he probably won't have a minute to spare for her.

"Come in."

Claire closes the door gently behind her and slips into the room. As always, she is awed to see her father writing at his desk.

"Am I disturbing you? Are you working?"

"I've finished. Sit down for a second, before your mother calls us for dinner."

Intimidated, Claire settles into the visitors' armchair. Her father observes her in silence, with a faint, enigmatic smile. The thick velvet curtains were drawn long ago, and the lamps glow with a dim, calming light. "This is a protected place," thinks Claire. She does not know how to ask him about *Les Mal-Aimés,* and in any event he does not give her the chance.

"Did you see Patrice's parents? Do they have any news?"

Claire tells him about her visit that afternoon and how they are afraid that he might be transferred to another camp. Her father seems upset.

"Poor boy, it's so unjust, what is happening to all those French prisoners in Germany . . . Patrice sent me a few letters during the summer . . . he's remarkably brave. A good man, a good man indeed. But you already know that, don't you?"

A voice from downstairs is calling them. Claire and her father get to their feet at the same time. Before stepping aside to let her go ahead, for a brief moment he touches her cheek with his fingers, ever so lightly.

"I'm glad you're going to marry him, he'll know how to make you happy. Because you can be so difficult, my little girl, so difficult . . . "

The news from the front is growing more and more alarming with each passing day. The German troops are putting up an unexpected resistance, and have the advantage on the Eastern front. At the avenue Théophile-Gautier, Claire is alone with her parents. Claude has gone to join General de Gaulle, Jean has enlisted with a unit of mountain infantrymen, Luce is looking after her children and her husband, Alain, the hero of the Vercors. It is Luce who asked Claire to postpone her departure. The two sisters have become acutely aware of how distraught their mother is: her fear never leaves her. Since October, François Mauriac has been receiving death threats from the extreme right wing under Darnand, the head of the Milice. Anonymous phone calls—menacing, vengeful, ringing day and night in the apartment. Once again they can expect the worst.

It is snowing today. Claire has decided not to go and visit Patrice's parents. She has put his photo on her night table and in the evening before she goes to sleep she gazes at it. Now she has the feeling she is close to him, and that she loves him. She has begun to write to him again. Long letters where she tells him about the harsh winter in Paris, and how at times she completely loses heart and has to fight against the feeling. Hoping to distract him, she talks about films she's seen, or the rehearsals for *Les Mal-Aimés* at the Comédie-Française. She has scrupulously written down the name of the director, Jean-Louis Barrault, and the three leads—Madeleine Renaud, Renée Faure, and Aimé Clariond.

Sitting at her table with a cigarette in one hand and a pen in the other, Claire stares at the snow that has covered her balcony and is still falling. How dreary: they shall have to clear the streets, and it will be hard to get around, and after that there will be mud. She's astonished that such things even bother her, when really she should really be in Belfort. She feels a burst of anger: she shouldn't have listened to her sister; her place is not here in the family apartment but there, where there is fighting and where she would not even have time to be afraid. Here her family's fear is spreading to her, gnawing away at her will to act. She puts down her pen, lights another cigarette. In a short while she'll go into the drawing room: it will be time for the news on the wireless. Besides, it's the only place where they keep the logs burning permanently. At least she'll be warm.

Tuesday, December 19, 1944

On Saturday the Germans began a major offensive on the border between Luxembourg and Belgium. They're advancing. It seems they have obtained considerable reinforcements in men and material. So how can we not be worried, awfully worried. We thought the Germans had no more strength; they were merely regrouping and stockpiling.

We really didn't need this. It's dreadful!

Even if we eventually manage to halt their attack, I can't help but think about all the bloodshed, all the villages that will be destroyed, and the reprisals that will ensue. I think about the thousands of desperate people, and all those people in France who are still hoping for a German victory. I think about this never-ending war, and Patrice's despair.

There are no words to describe the tenderness and sadness I am feeling, thinking about him just now. It's so unfair! He left his camp to go to Lübeck, and now they are on top of each other. He cannot help but think of me and wonder if I am waiting for him, because he won't be getting any letters. I wish he would return. I want to marry him and live quietly in the shadow of his love.

It's impossible to make any plans, alas.

And then there's this new weapon everyone has been talking

about for a while now, without actually believing in it: we're so afraid. And we're afraid of this *maquis brun*,[3] ready to attack at the first sign from Darnand. We're afraid of the Germans who are still in the west of France.

I'm afraid for Papa, because Darnand's men will kill him if Maurras is condemned to death—and he will be.

The future seems bleak, and this Christmas will probably be the most horrible one we've had all these years.

Claire closes her notebook. Because she can write in her diary what she will not allow herself to write to Patrice, and what she keeps silent from her parents, and because in her family it's considered bad form to complain, a thought has slowly formed, an absolute imperative: she must join her section in Alsace.

[3] Fascist underground movement.

Wednesday, December 27, 1944

Here I am again in Paris! Hard to imagine, but it's true. There's no point in crying because that's the way it had to be. On Christmas Day, when I was getting warm by the stove in our room, Minko came in and told me he needed an ambulance urgently.

So I drove all night and arrived in Paris at daybreak. What a reception at the FRC! As a result, I'm in Paris now and I don't know what I shall do.

Back to Christmas evening.

The Christmas Mass was dreary. It should have been marvelous, in a little church in a little Alsatian village, but it was ruined because the organ was hiccupping and the hymns were so pathetic you could weep. I couldn't help but think that this Christmas was even sadder than all the others, and about all the people who were dying on this freezing night; I thought about all the prisoners, and my poor Patrice's despair, and I know I prayed for him, and prayed that this horrible war would end.

No sooner had the mass finished than we were crammed into two ambulances and taken to another village where a whole group of officers was waiting for us to celebrate Christmas with dignity. The moon was magnificent, and our little trip left me with a good memory, how we were all squeezed together and singing. When we were dancing I thought, What if the Germans attack? At around six o'clock, a man came in and went to confer in a low voice with the others and an officer came to tell me there was an alert. And we all had to leave, almost in a rush.

Fortunately the night was short, because it was dreadful. I don't think I've ever been so cold in my life. I will always remember the Christmas sky on the following morning. Everything was so beautiful that I felt happy, almost strong.

Just before lunch, someone tapped me on the shoulder. I turned around and there was Minko.

"Here's the situation," he said. "My battalion is a kilometer from here. There's every chance of a German offensive and I don't have an ambulance."

All during lunch, which he stayed to share with us, I was wondering what to do. The girls were urging me to accept. In short, at the end of the meal I went to find our officer and asked him to tell our commander that I was leaving.

We quickly stowed our kit in Minko's vehicle. We'd already been driving for miles before I began to realize what I had done.

It was a good trip, despite the cold. The moon was magnificent, and I loved watching it roll past the trees. So I took the same road De Gaulle had taken, and I saw the same landscape, and he actually overtook us on his way back from the front. They stopped us any number of times because of him. We passed a burning car and I said, I just hope that's not the General's car. It wasn't, it was De Lattre de Tassigny's, he hadn't heard the warnings from the FFI, and a bullet set his fuel tank on fire.

We got to Paris at around eight o'clock.

Today the news from the front is good, and morale has improved. It seems the Germans have been brought to a halt.

I want to leave again.

Claire has gotten into the convenient habit of copying certain passages from her journal when she writes to Patrice. Not everything.

There's no point in talking about charming Minko who, unlike her fiancé, is a free man and is fighting. She turns Minko into an anonymous officer. Should she tell Patrice that on her own initiative she left her post to go and fetch an ambulance in Paris? Some people in the Red Cross might see this as a misdeed . . . and she might be temporarily suspended from her position. Would he even understand what's at stake . . . To be on the safe side, Claire goes no further in her story than Christmas night; she stresses her words of tenderness, tells him how eager she is for him to return, describes her dreams of the future, where he is more important than anything. The sentences come easily; she likes writing love letters. "Much more than receiving them," she thinks, amused.

Claire has just come out of the Jasmin métro station and is hurrying down the rue Ribera. In the overcrowded métro she almost threw up. All the people, and animals, and heavy perfume, it was disgusting, and you could practically smell the passengers' fear. She has been obsessed by the possibility of a migraine since she left the cinema, and it spoiled the hours she spent in the Café de la Paix with Martine and her fiancé.

For the last two days, the country has been gripped by a cold spell. In Paris the thermometer indicates zero; meteorologists predict that the situation will only get worse all through the month of January. The winter will be certainly as devastating as the winter of 1940. Claire cannot help but see this as a bad omen. Contrary to what she thought the day before, the German offensive in the Ardennes has not been halted, and a collective terror is spreading. An hour from now General de Gaulle will address the nation with his New Year's greetings. What will he say in his speech? Everyone in France will be waiting, like Claire, to listen to him on the wireless.

Back at home, Claire knocks on the door to her mother's bedroom and finds her lying in bed without even a book or some sewing at hand. A single lamp has been lit, and the curtains have not been drawn. This is not like her; Claire worries she might be ill.

"Don't you feel well, Mama?"

Claire is immediately alarmed by the way her mother shakes

her head, and by her pained expression. She thinks she understands: "Has there been another telephone call?"

"No."

In a weak voice her mother says, "Now they call at night."

There is so much anxiety in her voice that Claire sits at her
bedside, takes her hand and covers it with kisses. A fine, delicate hand, carefully groomed, fragrant with citronella eu de toilette. This hand, long ago, knew how to calm a fever or a childhood terror.

"The Sûreté is taking these threats very seriously . . . "

"You're not alone in the house, Mama."

"Weren't you supposed to go out with your sister?"

"I don't feel like it anymore. You must get up now, the
General will be on the air soon."

Claire kisses her mother's forehead, and places a blanket for
her across the chair. Then she goes back to her room to get
another pack of cigarettes.

> We have been wounded, but we are on our feet!
> The enemy is before us! The enemy who, to the west, to the
> east, and to the south, has gradually retreated, but still threatens,
> standing before us in a fit of rage, and in the year to come, 1945,
> they will waste no time in playing their final trumps.
> In the light of such fierce determination, all of France is aware
> of the new ordeals awaiting both our country and our allies.
> But all of France understands that through an enhanced war
> effort fate is giving us the opportunity to regain our place of
> eminence . . .

General de Gaulle's voice echoes in the silence of the drawing room, the building, the neighborhood, as if every man and
woman had gathered around their wireless, in their shared
need to listen. Claire can hear her parents breathing, sitting in
their armchairs with their backs to her; her sister Luce coughs
discreetly, kneeling next to her by the fireplace, where two logs
have just burned down. Neither sister wants to place another

log on the fire for fear of making noise. They strain to hear, not to miss a single word. From time to time, they exchange an incredulous glance, fear struggling with hope. Both of them are smoking, trying to keep the smoke away from their parents.

Men of France, women of France, may your thoughts unite over France! More than ever she needs to be loved and served by all of us; we are her children. She so deserves it!

After the General's voice, trembling with emotion, comes La Marseillaise. A few more seconds of silence in the drawing room, and all through the building, as if all the inhabitants were listening to the echo of the speech in their own minds. Then there comes a jazz tune from the floor above, and the sound of doors opening and slamming, a few words spoken near the elevator. Mechanically, Claire adds a huge log to the fireplace. She is vaguely aware of her father switching off the wireless and leaving the drawing room without a word.

What a sad way to end the year!

General de Gaulle has just spoken on the wireless: not a single word of hope for the new year, other than the fact that the enemy is prepared to come up with anything, and that everyone in France will be called on to fight, and we have still more suffering and tears in store.

Yesterday I was full of hope that the end was near. This evening I am desperate once again. I imagine the worst atrocities. I imagine the gas, and I'm afraid.

I was supposed to go to the Opéra this evening with Luce, but because Mama is so afraid, I have given up on the idea. She is afraid for Papa, afraid he will get another telephone call like the one Luce answered on Christmas night. A voice saying Papa will be assassinated within the two weeks to come if he goes on writing in Le Figaro.

How can I possibly be happy this evening?

I wish Patrice would come back. Don't I have the right to that happiness? If he were here, he would give me confidence, he would restore my faith in life.

I will love him . . . I will love him . . . "

A spring shower takes Claire by surprise as she is crossing the Pont Alexandre-III. She is dressed in a midseason suit with a jersey knit draped over her shoulders, and her legs are bare. She does not realize that the people she passes in the street are still wearing coats, for it is cold and rainy. She is walking like a robot, to the rhythm of the words: "I will love him." Just as she is about to come out onto the Esplanade des Invalides, she runs out of breath and collapses onto a bench, suddenly overwhelmed by the absurdity of her presence in Paris.

Yesterday she was in the south of France, in Cannes, with the Red Cross and the Allied armies. Yesterday she was working, dancing with officers every night, going to watch the sunrise on the coast. Yesterday she was free.

But then the call came, with its mixture of dread and anticipation: Patrice was liberated at the beginning of April, 1945, and he has just reached his parents' apartment and, he is there waiting for her. Claire told herself that she was ready. But his homecoming is so abstract, so far from her and the life she has been leading . . . She remembers how she used to talk about Patrice. Right from the start she informed her admirers that she was engaged, soon to be married. This allowed her to prevent any lighthearted flirtations from going too far, and to keep anyone who hoped to marry her from pointless pain and disappointment. Some of them warned her: "You don't love him!" To which she replied, "I've made a commitment."

"That's a typical wartime sort of commitment. You can break an engagement . . . "

It has stopped raining; only now does Claire realize she's been walking in the rain, and she's wet. The wooden bench has left a damp spot on her beige skirt. She glances at her watch and sees that she is late, but she cannot move. When she finally gets to her feet it is not because she has made any kind of decision, but rather because she has begun to tremble from the cold.

In the lobby of the building where Patrice's parents live a huge wall mirror sends her image back to her. Her suntanned face, her bare legs, and her midseason suit make her look as if she had just come back from vacation and had never known the war. She is bound to look out of place, they'll get the wrong impression. Something compels her back out onto the sidewalk, and she has an animal desire to flee, until she hears someone calling her name, and she turns around and sees Patrice waving to her from the balcony on the fourth floor.

Patrice is waiting for her on the landing. Claire only has time to see that he is in tears and that, in the doorway, his parents are crying, too. He takes her in his arms.

"Laurent stepped on a land mine, in Germany."

Claire observes the despair of this family, soon to be her own, through a haze of stunned distress. She cannot find the words to convey her sorrow; all she can do is weep, too, over the death of Patrice's favorite younger brother. They had celebrated his twenty-second birthday at the beginning of the year; she had admired his courage and patriotism. She hardly hears what Patrice is trying to tell her, in a voice she doesn't recognize. He is still holding her; she wonders who this stranger can be. She feels nothing at his touch, as if she were made of stone. His parents have begun to speak to her and now she can hear better. They tell her how much Laurent loved her, how proud he was at the thought of becoming her brother-in-law. They insist that her sweet presence will be a solace to them. Marriage is mentioned several times. Then it all goes very quickly, her thoughts in a whirl, and she understands that in the light of this disaster she will never be able to break her engagement.

Patrice insists on taking her home. In the métro, Claire pleads a migraine in order to take refuge in silence. Patrice stands by her side, sorrowful, stiff, ill at ease. He asks no questions about Claire herself or her activity with the Red Cross. Claire coolly notes the fact that he has lost a great deal of weight: his ghost-like appearance has hardly improved his looks. Still silent, they walk down the rue Ribera. Outside number 38 Avenue Théophile-Gautier, he kisses her on the cheek and leaves her with a terse, "See you tomorrow."

"So, how is he?"
Her mother came out of the drawing room when she heard the sound of the key in the lock. The sight of her daughter's pale face and distraught air are immediate cause for alarm. She asks her question again. Claire would like to throw herself in her mother's arms, confess that she no longer wants to marry Patrice, that their meeting was horrible; she would like to beg for her protection. But how can she explain something she herself does not understand? Tears flow down her cheeks, and she hears herself saying, "Laurent has just been killed, in Germany."
Her tears are as much for Patrice's return as for the young man's death.

That evening, in the darkness of her bedroom, she reviews the film of her day and bitterly concludes that her life, her real life, is over. As far as everyone else is concerned she is already married, even if a period of mourning will mean delaying the ceremony. Her parents were devastated to learn of the tragedy that has befallen this family—their friends—and not for a moment do they suspect that Claire might have changed, that four years of war have altered her feelings. They are ready to welcome Patrice with open arms and offer him all the affection he is entitled to expect.

Claire leaves her bed and opens the French doors. Although the night is cool, she goes out on the balcony and leans on the railing. Five stories below her the street is deserted. With a strange detachment she muses that it would be so easy to jump into the void. She sees a body, in her nightgown, lying on the pavement. Perhaps in the building across the way someone would see her jump and scream with horror. A scream that would rouse her family and neighbors from their sleep; a scream that would haunt them for a very long time. They would all think it was an accident. A young woman who is about to be married does not take her own life.

S ummer has come, the first since the end of the war, and Paris is splendid once again: the tourists have returned and the streets are bursting with joie de vivre. At least that is how Claire is feeling as she hurries down the Avenue Mozart. It seems to her that all these women in flowered dresses, arms and legs bared, are as happy as she is, like the old men resting on public benches, or the children playing ball. She does not see the sky clouding over, the signs of imminent rain. For her this is the most beautiful day of the summer. She feels alive again; she is free.

Rue Ribera, rue François-Gérard, avenue Théophile-Gautier. Claire is in a hurry to get back to the apartment and write down the story of these last months—to find out why she feels so cheerful. She has not touched her diary since December, 1944, and now it is waiting for her to get it out one last time.

> Wednesday, August 22, 1945
> I don't know where to begin.
> This evening, after all these years, I am right back at the same point as before the war. I am free, I'm not going to marry Patrice! It took me days and days just to figure it out that, basically, I was not obliged to marry him.
> But I would like to give a brief account of my life.
> On March 5, I left for Fréjus as a driver, and then on to Cannes.
> I have marvelous memories of that time. I went out every day with Jean-Pierre—Pierrot to his friends—an adorable boy who fell madly in love with me. And I did nothing to stop him. I simply told him that I was waiting for Patrice who was in Germany, but I didn't tell him that I wasn't in love.

Pierrot and I went every evening to an American Navy Officers' Club. What a wonderful place—I'll never forget it, or the officers, all so handsome and friendly. They drank a great deal, played the piano, danced, etc. The setting was divine and before long I was a regular. The only problem was that I don't speak English! We always left the club terribly late and then we would drive around for the rest of the night. I'll never forget the beauty of Cap-d'Antibes. The next morning, I had to get up at seven o'clock for work. It goes without saying that I was perpetually exhausted.

One day the dispatch I'd been dreading more than anything arrived: Patrice was in Paris.

So I got ready to leave the Red Cross, saying I had to go back to Paris. But I was so reluctant and afraid that I stayed on for a few days. It was as if these were my last days of vacation, and I had to live them to the fullest. I was with Pierrot every day. We would drive endlessly, leaving the coast to head inland, or to watch the sunrise or sunset at such and such a place.

But on April 2 I took the airplane, and during the day I arrived at Patrice's home. I am sure that at that moment I did not love him; perhaps I even resented him for all the space that he had stolen, more or less—not from my heart but from my life.

The memory of that day, more than three months later, is still so powerful that Claire suddenly feels an icy chill. Once again she sees the rain, the family's sorrow, their pain on telling her of dear, kind Laurent's death. Once again she feels like a hunted, trapped beast. She is not in her bedroom, but stretched out on one of the sofas in the drawing room: her parents are having dinner with friends, and she is alone in the apartment. On the floor is a tray with fruit and iced tea. Through the open windows she can hear the cries of swallows, the faraway sounds of the city. The sight of the paintings on the walls, the presence of familiar furniture, the piano, her mother's beloved and ubiquitous knickknacks that so irritate her father—everything about the décor is calming. "It's all over, I'm free!" she says out loud. And goes on to pick up the story she had briefly interrupted, of that terrible month of April.

I was so unhappy I could have died, because it felt like—I was certain—I had lost everything. I would fall asleep and wake up again with an enormous lump of dread at the back of my throat, in my stomach, in my heart. Moreover, my family was watching my every move, my every word. I wanted to run away, screaming at the top of my lungs.

And then one day . . . But in the meantime there was the armistice on May 8. I had never felt so full of anguish as on that day. The night before, among a crowd that was going wild, I was on my way up the Champs-Elysées with Claude and Luce, and I was crying to myself, very silently, at the sight of the joy on everyone's face, a joy I could not share. What a sad, sad day of celebration.

Then one day I got a phone call from my section leader.

"Mauriac, you are leaving this afternoon for Germany."

"But Mademoiselle, I can't!"

Contrary to what I expected, she was very sweet and above all very clever: "I understand perfectly, but we need you in Germany. It will be very interesting," etc. I confess that when I put down the phone I immediately started thinking about departure. The next thing I knew I was standing in front of the head of the entire Red Cross.

"Come now, Mauriac, what are you going on about! You don't love him very much, that boy! You're no longer my girl if you don't get going!"

Etc.

In short, in the space of five minutes I decided to get going, and without further ado I went to Patrice's house and spoke to him about duty with a capital D., and so on.

I saw this trip to Germany as my last vacation before my wedding, a wedding that filled me with horror but which would have to take place and would take place.

I stayed in Germany for three months, three wonderful months. Extraordinary, meaningful work. I'll never forget all those prisoners we transported, how happy they were at last.

All the north of the country is magnificent. It's nothing like France. Everything seems bigger, grander, with a certain melancholy but much more beautiful. I shall never forget those vast forests with their immense trees, the pines so thickly forested, their trunks so close together that the sun could not enter; and those long roads with birch trees all along either side, and those endless expanses of pink heather, and the lakes surrounded by green trees, and the Elbe, and the sea, and those huge cities in ruins, Bremen, Hamburg . . .

In three months, I traveled nearly 20,000 kilometers.

I have had to wait until now in my profession as a driver to find out what it means to almost fall asleep at the wheel. It's the most dreadful thing, an excruciating effort with every passing moment. I remember one day when I had been driving all day and all night without stopping (we were going back and forth to the Russian zone), I had to ask the man who was with me to keep punching me, over and over.

Claire suddenly sits up when she hears the telephone ringing. For a split second she is reminded of how afraid they were in late 1944, early 1945, when her father was receiving anonymous death threats. That dark chapter of her life is over as well. She doesn't feel like answering, but the caller insists. What if one of her family has had an accident? The reflex of fear is rooted deep inside her.

With a trembling hand she lifts the receiver and immediately recognizes the voice. A voice she does not like, a voice she finds affected, sepulchral: Patrice's voice.

"Hello? May I speak to Mademoiselle Mauriac?"

"I'm sorry sir, she has gone away."

"Is she in the country at her grandmother's?"

"No, she left this afternoon for Germany."

The caller hangs up right away. Claire puts the phone down, her hands still trembling. She pictures Patrice, his humiliation, his stiffness, his acrimony. Has he already told his parents? How sad and disappointed they must be! Thinking about them she feels something like pity wash over her. But very quickly a fierce survival instinct compels her take hold of herself. It's all Patrice's fault, she reasons, he took advantage of his situation as a prisoner of war to force a commitment from her. Her only fault has been to have such a love of writing. She shouldn't have let herself go to the pleasure of writing love letters.

The church bells in Auteuil ring half past nine; Claire picks up her notebook. Outside, the sky is getting dark and a fine drizzle has begun to fall.

> It's raining this evening but I'm happy because I'm free. I cannot dwell on the pain Patrice is feeling, which must be tremendous . . . I'm terrible and I disgust myself, but I can't dwell on that, either.
> I'm still so young. I have to go to Berlin; I have everything to hope for from life. I mustn't be punished. I didn't know.

Claire closes her notebook, determined to forget Patrice. She thinks about calling her new friend Mistou—they'll be going to Berlin together. Mistou is very beautiful, always ready for a good time, and—important detail—an excellent driver. The two young women have just been assigned to Mobile Group Number 5 in charge of repatriating French prisoners still in Germany.

The ringing of the phone makes her jump. Claire doesn't want to risk hearing Patrice's voice again. Maybe someone told him she was still in Paris. Maybe he's calling back to demand a final confrontation. Their meeting that morning had been so difficult that she cannot bear the idea of a new discussion. She knows she is still vulnerable here in Paris; in Berlin she will be out of harm's way.

To drown out the sound of the ringing telephone she switches on the wireless. A jazz tune: her American officer friends have given her a taste for jazz, and she recognizes Louis Armstrong's trumpet. Since there's no one in the apartment, she turns the volume up all the way, throws open the doors of the drawing room, dining room, and hallway, and begins to dance. She's convinced a new life is beginning—an unknown, vibrant life, far from everything she has known up to now. To her the very name of the defeated city—Berlin—echoes with promise.

August 31, 1945
Dear Papa, dear Mama,
What a truly terrible thing Berlin is! You cannot imagine how bleak it is, this enormous city without a single house left standing. Worse yet—a thousand times worse—are the people of Berlin, living in cellars and dying of hunger.

I saw a man fall down in the street. The Belgians, who've been here for two weeks, told us that when they go into the houses to inspect them, they often find corpses—children, adults, who have just died. Moreover, there's a terrible epidemic of dysentery and people are dying like flies.

Today I spent the day in half-destroyed factories looking for workers who've disappeared. I don't need to tell you that it wasn't fun at all.

Just now at a station in the Russian sector, a soldier asked me for my watch—he wanted to exchange it for his. When I said no, he said he would pay me for it. Fortunately another Russian came over and when he saw that I was French he told the other fellow to leave me alone.

Tomorrow I have to get up at seven for the aviation camp.

I'm tired and everything I've seen has made me horribly sad. It's almost as if the people in Berlin weren't even human anymore.

It's eleven o'clock. Ten o'clock, your time.

It took us four days to get here because the others were driving like imbeciles.

The first night we slept in Liège and I had all the warning signs of a stomach upset. As you can imagine I was pretty miserable. The next day the heat was unbearable, we crossed the Ruhr. It took us all day, because everything is destroyed and the roads are all torn up. It was a series of towns sitting in the middle of open country, one after the other, separated only by factories. Cologne left an unbelievable impression on me. It must have been a magnificent city. Now all that's left is the river, which is very beautiful, and, above all, the Cathedral. From a distance it doesn't seem to have been too badly damaged, and the beauty and grandeur of it amidst all the ruins is unbelievable.

Here we have a frightful amount of work. We can forget about having fun, but at least our work will be truly useful.

If you drink the water you're dead. We eat only out of cans.

This morning when we woke up our morale wasn't very good, but now it's a lot better. It's all so tough and fascinating at the same time!

Hugs and kisses to my dear parents,

Claire Mauriac

French Red Cross – British Control Commission – D.P. Section – Berlin Area – B.A.O.R.

Claire closes the envelope for her parents. There's a plane leaving for Paris tomorrow, and someone on board will manage to get the letter to them. The passengers will be Frenchmen who had been conscripted into the *Service du Travail Obligatoire*— the Compulsory Work Service—and who served as hostages right up to the end, when the German army was in retreat. The ones who survived the capture of Berlin by the Soviet army were assimilated with the defeated and put in camps. Claire and the other newcomers have been told that finding them and obtaining their liberation is not an easy task.

Claire is sitting on a camp bed to write, her pad of paper on her knees. Around her, five young women are getting ready for bed. Since the Red Cross has not managed to find them any decent accommodation, for the time being they are housed in the erstwhile refectory of what was once a boys' school. It's temporary, and they know it, and are getting along with each other as best they can. Claire is the one having the hardest time adjusting to community life, but she is learning to be patient. Rolanne, a young woman who looked after her three days earlier when she had her upset stomach, is helping her. Moreover, all it takes for her to regain her courage is to look over at Rolanne, in the bed to her right. Rolanne, defeated by fatigue, has no trouble sleeping, despite the noise and conversations that are well above a whisper.

"There you go, yet another letter! Want to write to my parents while you're at it?"

Mistou, stretched out on her camp bed, is waiting for sleep, forcing a yawn. She is wearing elegant silk pajamas and has smeared her face with a thick cream that smells like cucumber. In spite of four days spent traveling from Paris to Berlin, the discomfort of their quarters, the absence of a bathroom, and the promiscuity of five other women, her beauty is flawless, as if it could be preserved forever. Claire smiles at her and pointing at Rolanne she says, "We should do the same."

There are no curtains or shutters in the refectory. It is getting dark with the declining day. Here and there flashlights are switched on. In the solitary tree in the former schoolyard, blackbirds are singing. Claire is astonished to find them there: how can they survive in this ruined city? Claire wants to forget the corpses she and Mistou and Rolanne have picked up; the horrible ghostly aspect of the handful of Berliners they have seen—because most of them are still hiding in cellars; the gangs of starving errant children involved in all sorts of trafficking; and above all the stubbornly silent women of Berlin, whose suffering is so visible: she is filled with fear and rebellion whenever she sees them. Claire and her companions have been getting help from one of them, a woman who speaks five languages, including French, English, and Russian. She translated their words without ever making the slightest personal comment, without allowing herself to communicate anything at all; she withdrew into herself, elsewhere. At the end of the day, when they gave the woman her share of American canned goods and a bottle of brandy, all she had to say was, "To the entire world we are *Trümmerweiber,* women from the ruins and the dirt." Then she went away, toward an unknown destination.

It is almost completely dark in the dormitory now, and the girls are beginning to fall silent. Outside, the blackbirds are still singing and their song helps Claire to banish the images of these two days in Berlin. It is a song of hope, and she wants to hear nothing else from now on.

September 10, 1945
Dear Mama,

I'm beginning to get used to the ruins, and life in Berlin is fascinating, provided you're not from Berlin.

The other day there was an amazing parade to celebrate the end of the war in Japan: a thousand Russians, a thousand Frenchmen, a thousand Englishmen, and a thousand Americans!

The Russian parade was incredible: they formed a solid wall, marching like a single man. You must have seen it at the cinema, but that's nothing like the real thing.

It was grand for us to see that the French had equal standing, just as many men and just as many flags. General Zhukov went by only a yard away from me, covered in medals like Goering.

Just across from us they played music from the four countries. You can imagine how overjoyed we were to hear "*Vous n'aurez pas l'Alsace et la Lorraine*" right there on the grand avenue where Hitler had so many of his big parades.

September 11, 1945
I just got your letter and the plane is leaving in an hour.

I am in a strange place, I tell you, at the hospital, at the bedside of a young Russian who has become a morphine addict after being severely wounded. During the night Rolanne really struggled with him. Fortunately he didn't have a revolver, but this morning he got hold of a knife. I didn't want to go in there alone, and I'm with Mistou. It's really a horrible sight.

We spend most of our time in the Russian zone. Day before yesterday we were in Leipzig. The Russians are charming people, but the missions in Lüneburg that used to take us one morning now take two days with them. You have to wait four hours to get a room, four hours to go into the camp, etc. In the beginning, you get really annoyed but then you make the most of it. We always take a Russian officer with us on our missions. Don't go talking about what I'm writing to you, because we're the only ones allowed into the Russian zone. The English, Americans, and French who can't go in there really envy us. Even the International Red Cross isn't allowed in there.

Fortunately at the gates to Berlin there are some terrific clubs, and we've had some swell evenings.

If you know anyone who has disappeared in Berlin or anywhere nearby, send me all the information. I spend a lot of my time working on this. Days and days on such requests, and often I get no results at all. It's terrible!

Yesterday I went to visit the Chancellery. I saw the study, Hitler's bedroom, and his shelter. I took a few pieces of marble from his desk. I'll go again, because I'd like to get a big piece.

We're having fine weather but it's cold. Right now in this hospital room I'm freezing.

My Mama, very big hugs and kisses to you and Papa.
WRITE!

Two days ago Claire and Mistou moved into the nicest room on the fifth floor of a building located at 96 Kurfürstendamm; all the broken windowpanes have just been replaced. Workers have been fixing up the adjacent bathroom, and before long the two young women will have a bathtub and heating: it is beginning to look as if it will be a cold winter in Berlin. The Red Cross has already given them shapkas and long, elegant navy blue coats, with masculine tailoring and a removable fur lining. Claire would never have thought it possible to find such comfort in the ruined city. Their section comrades are housed on a different floor, in smaller, hastily furnished rooms. They drew lots, fair and square, and with a lucky roll of the dice Claire and Mistou won the privilege of inhabiting this room, baptized, who knows why, "the floozies' room." After numerous conjectures the two friends decided it might be due to the fact that the bed has a canopy, or maybe it's because of the curtains, or the walls papered in candy pink and sky blue satin; the taste is so atrocious that it is downright delightful.

A quick knock on the door and Rolanne appears.

"Come on, we're going to meet the inhabitants of the other floors. They've brought out something to drink in our honor . . . "

Claire hesitates; she has been savoring the prospect of a quiet moment to herself, the first she's had since they arrived in Berlin two weeks earlier. Rolanne waits patiently for her to make up her mind.

"Oh, come on," she insists in a gentle voice.

Her calm face and regular features reflect a kindliness which works wonders on Claire. Claire gets to her feet without a glance at the mirror hanging above the bed. Ever since she left Paris, she seems to have given up all interest in her appearance.

October 15, 1945
Dear Papa, dear Mama,
A dreary, rainy Sunday. This weather is truly in harmony with the ruins of Berlin: you don't even think about being down in the dumps.

The day before yesterday I set off to help organize a camp where the trains with the Alsatians would arrive. For a day and a half we offloaded, unpacked, organized and stored thousands of items of clothing, shoes, etc. I finished last night at seven o'clock. Although they'd announced the train several days before it still hadn't come in. I drove for hours through the night, I love these nighttime journeys; the other drivers hate them.

I read in the papers that Papa was in Brussels. How is his new play going?

We are living in a big, four-story house—a madhouse, never a dull moment!

On the first floor: rooms of Belgian and French women. Offices, rooms, dining room, etc.

Second floor: quarters for the French officers.

Third floor: apartment for the personnel of the Displaced Persons Section.

Fourth floor: several bedrooms, including mine, which I share with Mistou. For two days now we've had heating, and as of today I can take a bath in my own bathtub, because Mistou and I have a bathroom.

I might leave tomorrow for the Polish zone . . .

The other day, after I wrote to you, I had a terrible upset stomach, and vomited six or seven times. Fortunately I was able to lie down.

Since then I've been fairly tired. I'm much better today, I get the feeling it was the drive last night. Just imagine going for hours along a straight road between two walls of pine trees, it's pitch black, with just our dim little headlights. We were alone in the ambulance but traveling in convoy: a light vehicle with two officers, my ambulance, another one behind me, and a big truck.

We were driving some Russians, their officer got into the car with the French officers, pulled out his revolver, and kept it in his hand. Isn't it incredible how trusting they are!

But today the four Russian-speaking French officers in our house went to have lunch with these gentlemen. A very, very good sign.

There's a lot of talk of war here. But we talk about it in such a simple way that no one is really afraid. It's just that you don't feel like making plans for the future. It would simplify a lot of things, not to die too old . . .

Kisses to you both and hugs from the bottom of my heart.

Claire resisted the temptation to say anything more about the strange, oppressive uneasiness she's feeling. She has decided to hide from her parents, from all of her family, those moments when she succumbs to despondency, those dark brooding days following a mission; better not to dwell on what they have begun to find out, about the death camps, and the mass extermination of the Jews.

But this evening she's particularly upset by the news that a German woman has died from septicemia, and she was helpless to save her. Like so many others, the woman had been raped several times by Soviet soldiers, and she'd tried to have an abortion. A mere handful of women, treated by the Red Cross, have begun to talk about the horrors of the capture of Berlin and the Soviet occupation. Claire cannot understand why the Allies took so long to reach Berlin, and sometimes she says indignantly to French officers, "Why did General Eisenhower let the Red Army fight the final battle? Why did no one object to his decision?" "It was war," is more or less the only answer she managed to get. At the beginning of her time in Berlin, Claire swore loud and clear that she had no pity for the Germans, and she swore she would never forgive them for the atrocities they had committed; whatever they were going through was surely justice. Now she can no longer say this. The woman who had acted as interpreter that time has come back to work for them. Her name is Hilde, and Rolanne has been trying, ever so slowly, to win her over. What Claire has been finding out about this woman's past makes a far greater impression on her than any of the rumors beginning to circulate about a possible war between the Americans and the Russians.

Rolanne has begun to get a good grasp of the fractured geography of the defeated country, so she has been trying to explain it to Mistou and Claire. Mistou is busy putting polish on her toenails, while Claire lies daydreaming on her bed.

"Roughly two-thirds of Germany is occupied by the Soviets, including Berlin, right? Nevertheless, the Allies have managed to keep three small zones in Berlin, three sectors actually: a French sector, an American sector, and a British sector. Our building is located in the British sector. Do you follow?"

But Mistou is leafing through an old fashion magazine, and Claire is looking gloomy. Rolanne gives up on her explanations. She knows that Claire might well begin to act childishly, to rant about how she doesn't like the English, they burned Joan of Arc at the stake and poisoned Napoleon and she would rather be in the French sector. And yet Claire knows very well that the British sector is the one that is located closest to the train stations where the convoys of prisoners arrive, and the Red Cross is working with the Displaced Persons Section, the organism in charge of locating and repatriating all the French prisoners spread throughout the devastated country.

Because she is a loyal friend, Rolanne offers to make tea and goes downstairs to the kitchen, on the floor where the other girls live.

The building at 96 Kurfürstendamm is home to a number of people who work very well together and share the same ideals. The French and the Belgian Red Cross workers have excellent relations: the women collaborate, regardless of nationality. They share missions, take their meals together. The French officers often join them; like their leader, Léon de Rosen, they are hardly over thirty. All of them take the search for displaced persons very seriously, and they serve as escorts for the Red Cross convoys. One of them in particular, a French officer of Russian origin, is particularly gifted at cajoling the Soviet authorities.

Claire decides to write to her parents. Her mother has been urging her to come back to Paris and is she annoyed with Claire for not giving a definite answer or date in her letters. In spite of her daughter's descriptions, she seems unable to grasp the exact nature of Claire's life in Berlin. Claire, with a tinge of bitterness, senses that they still don't take her work seriously; her father seems to have forgotten her. Not a single letter, just a few words now and again scribbled hastily at the bottom of the page.

She pulls out her pad of paper and settles down at the inlaid desk that has become her usual spot.

October 23, 1945

Dear Mama,

Yesterday I went to get the ashes of eighty-seven Frenchmen the Germans had executed by firing squad. We picked them up at the crematorium in Brandenburg. They were all very young Frenchmen, sentenced to death for sabotage or espionage. You cannot imagine the effect this had on me. A little urn, a name, a date: all that remains of a human being.

We are waiting for the trains to arrive with the Alsatians any day now.

I don't know exactly when I'll be back. Yesterday they decided we should go back at the end of the month, but now they want to keep us for these trains with the Alsatians.

They have to have the ambulances here, and if we leave, we'll be replaced, something we don't want. There is still a lot of work to do, and it would be really upsetting not to finish what we've begun.

Still, life here is beginning to be quite pleasant, and the house is really very comfortable. Winter is bound to be tough for the local people, but not for us in any case.

Morale is fairly good and I keep busy. I cannot say I am bursting with joy, but it's not like I'm dying of sorrow either!

The weather is beautiful, and it's very cold.

Hugs and kisses, dear Mama.

Rolanne has just come in and sets a tray down on the bed. She pours three cups of tea and takes one over to Claire. Claire gives her a grateful smile. Rolanne is the only one who doesn't tease her about the mysterious moments of sadness that overwhelm her at times; she doesn't probe, and all it takes is a gaze or the pressure of her hand for Claire to know that she is there for her. She seems to understand that Claire can't really control these moods, and she doesn't judge her.

"We're invited for dinner with the British officers," says Mistou. "Shall we go? The food is dreadful but there'll be dancing afterwards. Say, can I have an answer, girls?"

October 24, 1945
Dear little Mama,
It looks like we'll be staying here for the time being. This annoys me only for your sake, because as for me, I really don't have a clue what I would do in Paris. I would certainly have to see Patrice again and I honestly don't think I have the courage. I've had no news from him, and even when I'm alone I don't dare think about it. The other day I sent a note to his mother.

Here I'm leading a life outside of life. It's been that way for several years now. I always think I've reached the end, that that's it, but it never is.

What am I to make of the time I have left to live—I don't know.

You mustn't think that I am sad. I love this life I'm leading precisely because I know it will not last forever.

I received the gloves and the rest of the package. Thank you so much.

I had my photograph taken by a very good photographer.

Dear Mama, I give you a very big hug.

Claire is writing on a corner of the table in the kitchen. Next to her two women from the Belgian Red Cross, ambulance drivers, too, are busy making very strong cocktails, chatting noisily. They taste their drinks with increasing frequency, and they're a bit tipsy, but Claire pays them no mind. She is astonished by what she has just written to her mother. Never before has she confided in her so simply and naturally, as if she had finally found the words to express both what she fears and what she appreciates about her life at the moment— a temporary life, as if suspended in time. Which it is. She is afraid to go back to Paris. She is afraid to be caught up for good in a life where everything has been laid out in advance. It really has nothing to do with Patrice. With a chilling lucidity Claire realizes that she is destined to get married to someone like Patrice. She imagines her future children, the regular visits to her parents, the vacations in country homes. She now knows that the war has enabled her to avoid being caught in a rut, that she needs to feel useful, perhaps even indispensable. In Caen, then in Béziers, Fréjus, Cannes, and now Berlin, she has felt alive. In the eyes of others she is Claire Mauriac and not just someone's daughter or fiancé.

"Phew, it stinks of booze in here."

The newcomer in the kitchen is a young woman five feet tall with a round face and domed forehead, who was recently promoted section leader of the French Red Cross in Berlin. The energy and efficiency with which she has taken charge of her group are cause for universal admiration, including the officers on the second floor. Her name is Jeanine, but because of her size and slender shape, all the inhabitants of 96 Kurfürstendamm have baptized her "Plumette."

The two Belgian nurses try to explain that they've been making cocktails, but Plumette doesn't let them finish.

"I've been informed that there's a convoy of Alsace-Lorraine prisoners arriving, it would be stupid for you to get drunk now."

She turns to Claire: "Get the ambulance ready with all the equipment. You're going back to the station with Mistou."

November 2, 1945

Dear Mama,

Your parcel hasn't arrived yet because there haven't been any planes, given the bad weather in Paris.

Here the sky is blue, and it's not cold.

I got back yesterday from three days of making the rounds. Nothing special to relate, all we brought back were death certificates, all our patients had died. In Halle, we discovered a cemetery where every day for three years, a German man buried twenty bodies of people beheaded by ax: French, Belgians, etc.

We went through thirty-two villages occupied by the Russians. Wherever we went there was music blaring full volume, in the village square from six o'clock in the morning until midnight. Wherever you looked there were great big painted portraits (childish drawings!) of Stalin and the others, red stars, both tiny and enormous, and huge red flags. At night, everything is surrounded by little colored lamps.

The trainloads of Alsatians are still arriving.

November 7

Finally there's a plane leaving tomorrow!

The weather is fine here. Why are you having such bad weather in Paris?

More trainloads of Alsatians. The day before yesterday all the way from Riga. That's how it goes here.

We were notified at seven o'clock in the evening. It took me five minutes to fill the tank, twenty minutes to load the ambulance with the parcels from the FRC, then we set off at night with the added difficulty of trying to find a train station on the other side of town (somewhere within twenty-five kilometers) in the middle

of the ruins, and then the tracks. While the Russian-speaking officer went to negotiate with the Russians who were accompanying
the convoy, I stood for two hours in the cold and dark waiting on
the goodwill of these gentlemen. There was another girl with me,
and she wanted to turn her ambulance around. The engine got
stuck (you couldn't see a thing) in a switch. Impossible to get it out
of there, and the car was right up against the tracks. Naturally
along came a locomotive. Fortunately it wasn't going fast and was
able to stop in time. It took six Germans and a lever to get the car
out of there. Finally above all, along came a crowd of Alsatians and
we were able to give them their parcels. Like every time, we were
the first French women they had seen in so long, and you can
imagine how elated they were.

But the officer came back empty-handed: the Russians didn't
want to give us the men, five of whom were in very serious condition, the other twenty lightly wounded.

We went home again feeling defeated because it meant a death
sentence for the first five at any rate. We had dinner and decided
to try again the next day.

So off I went again at eight o'clock with another officer, a
much cleverer sort, and this time we had to go clear to the other
side of Berlin because the train had moved. We distributed the
parcels. The Alsatians, nearly all of whom were from Strasbourg,
began weeping tears of joy. At last someone was showing them
they cared! You really have to have seen these trains to understand. These poor boys had all suffered so much that they'd
reached a point where they'd lost all hope. The Russians have
been treating them no better than the Germans. No food or
clothing, and it has been snowing since the end of September.
Not only have they had no news from home, they've had no news
at all, not a word from France. They were all sickly and thin, with
huge grave eyes, and they hadn't had a laugh (because they never
laugh in that part of the world, I saw what it was like in
Pomerania) for years. So imagine, now they suddenly see French
ambulances and French girls, bringing them cigarettes and a
bunch of other things! One of the Alsatians said to me, "Last
night when we saw the ambulances we said, We're going to be all
right, men, it's the French Red Cross, and we cried."

In the meantime, and it took forever, the Russian-speaking
French officer was busy palavering and finally got what he wanted

by inviting the Russians to lunch. I got down to loading the five who were in bad condition. Their eyes began to shine with joy when I told them that they were going to have a warm bed and some hot food and as soon as they were better there would be a plane taking them to France and in three hours they'd be home.

I helped the others into a second ambulance. There was one who was so weak that he was sobbing.

After a good bath we got them to bed and they said, "Thank you sister, we won't forget you."

This morning I took them some chocolate and cigarettes and when I told them I wasn't a sister, they said, "For us you are. A sister and Father Christmas, too."

You have to admit, Mama dear, it's an incredible sort of job I've got, as much for my own sake as for France. And you have to admit it might be worth staying on for a while!

Another train was headed our way but it stopped a hundred and fifty kilometers from here so two drivers went to meet them. There the prisoners will be dressed as Frenchmen, and they'll be free of the Russians; the most exhausted ones will be put onto a hospital train.

On my way back from the hospital today, I had to pick up a woman who'd been knocked down by a Russian truck. It happened right before my eyes. It's the third time since I got to Germany and every single time these German women have died in my ambulance.

On Monday we're going back into the Russian zone. On Sunday we'll have a huge party for Armistice Day.

Once again, Mama, please excuse this letter which I won't take the time to re-read because it is (would you believe!) four o'clock in the morning.

I got the perfume. Thanks ever so much, it's wonderful.

Mistou is leaving for Paris on Monday, and she'll be bringing you some photos of me.

I hug you as tight as I can, and Papa, too, he's forgotten me, but I still love him as much as ever.

Your little Claire.

With two or three brisk movements Claire undresses, places her uniform on a hanger, and pulls on her pajamas. She switches off the night light which allowed her to write without waking Mistou, and slips at last between the sheets.

They share the double bed; Mistou sleeps on her back, breathing regularly, and Claire detects a faint smile on her lips. They get along very well, people take them for sisters, or at the least longtime friends. Claire reckons that one year of war is the equivalent of ten years of normal life. The ordeals she has been through with Mistou, Rolanne, and Plumette, their shared moments of joy and triumph, have brought them much closer than simple family ties would have.

"I have to sleep now," thinks Claire.

But she cannot sleep, and she begins to toss and turn. Her restless thoughts give her no respite, scurrying at a dizzying speed in every direction. In a few seconds her happy, almost euphoric, mood has given way to waves of panic that make it hard to breathe.

She didn't tell her mother everything.

She didn't tell her the most important thing.

She made a painstaking report on the last forty-eight hours spent rescuing the Alsatians who were held captive by the Soviets; she insisted on the failure of their attempts the first day, and how they decided to try again the next day, and finally succeeded on every count. Without their stubbornness, twenty-five men would have been doomed to certain death: French Alsatians who had been enrolled by force in the German army, the *malgré-nous*, as they were called. Without going into any details, she did mention a second Russian-speaking officer. Nor did she really go into, or hardly at all, how decisive his role turned out to be.

Claire thinks of her letter as a game a child might play, one of those drawings where somewhere in the foliage of a tree or in the clouds or in an animal's fur the main figure, the subject of the riddle, has been carefully hidden.

She goes back over every minor detail of that evening in the kitchen with the girls when, along with Rolanne and the first

Russian-speaking officer, she had felt so dejected, so helpless. All three of them felt it, it was agonizing. And then another officer who also worked in the Displaced Persons Section had come down to join them.

Claire can still hear his confident, cheerful voice telling her, as if it were a simple Sunday stroll: "Well, we'll just have to go back there tomorrow morning first thing. You have my word, we'll get them all out of there." Claire had immediately sprung to her feet: "I'll go with you."

"I should hope so." Claire knows that it was at that very moment, with those simple words, that they at last confessed their love. Because in her insomnia Claire is forced to acknowledge what she had refused to see: she fell in love with that Russian-speaking Frenchman the moment they met.

"Will you stop it with your St. Vitus's dance? You've woken me up with all your fidgeting!"

Claire sits up abruptly and, taking her head in her hands she says, "Goodness gracious, Mistou, what is going to become of me?"

H is name is Yvan Wiazemsky, born in 1915 in St. Petersburg, and his family, like thousands of others, emigrated at the time of the Revolution. For a long time they were stateless, and then in the 1930s they obtained French nationality. Wia, as everyone calls him, was mobilized as soon as war was declared. He was immediately taken prisoner. Five years of hardship in the camps had not put a dent in his confidence and exuberance. Liberated by the Soviets, he fought at their side until he met up with Léon de Rosen, then went on to become both his right-hand man and his best friend. He is the most popular French officer at 96 Kurfürstendamm, adored by men and women alike. He's always the first to volunteer for a mission, and the first to throw a party. He speaks seven languages fluently including Russian, French, English, and German, and he knows how to make friends wherever he goes, both in the camp where he was a prisoner and in Allied-occupied Berlin. These qualities have made him an excellent negotiator, and the girls often ask him to come along when they are on their way to rescue some Frenchmen in the Soviet zone.

The moment Claire moved into the building she could not help but notice him. He was the one who organized a little reception to welcome the French Red Cross; he was the one responsible for the constant to and fro between the floors. By the end of the first party everyone felt as if they had known each other for a long time, and with this impression came a sincere desire to work together. There had been dancing, singing, and drinking, and a great number of toasts drunk to the end of the war, the return of the prisoners, and the reconciliation of nations. "It's too much," thought Claire: to her he was some sort of Martian. "He's got us all in his pocket! We won't get bored with him around," said Mistou, bemused, and Rolanne sighed dreamily, "He's so charming . . . " Later on the Belgian women told the French women that Wia was an actual prince, and his family was one of the oldest in Russia. "Big deal . . . " had been Claire's only remark. Nevertheless, she had to admit that he was pleasant, easy to get along with, and a good comrade. She did not seem to notice that Wia seemed quite taken, and was trying very hard to please her.

One morning, when she was on the second floor in Léon de Rosen's office, reading an article in a French newspaper about a trip her father had taken to Switzerland, Wia asked, "Who's this François Mauriac?"

"Go on, Wia, you're having us on! You must know who François Mauriac is!" said Léon de Rosen indignantly.

"No, I don't. So, who is he?" Claire began to laugh irrepressibly for the first time since she arrived in Berlin—what delightful ignorance! She found herself sitting on the floor, rocking with laughter, and merely grew more hysterical when Wia, whom his friend Léon finally filled in, tried to apologize. "Don't you read books?" asked Claire through her giggles as she tried to calm down. "Never!" Off she went again, her hilarity a mystery to the two men.

When Claire left the office to go back up to her floor, she felt like singing with joy in the stairway: at last she had met a man who was interested in her for her own sake, interested in her and no one else; a man who did not even know she had such a famous father; a man for whom literature and books had absolutely no importance. A novel situation, and enchanting. This Wia fellow truly was a Martian, just as she had suspected. From that moment on, she could sense when he was paying attention to her.

On one of their missions with Mistou and Plumette, when the Soviets were denying they had any French prisoners, he once again displayed his unflagging determination not to go home empty-handed. They were over a hundred kilometers from Berlin, in a devastated zone, without a single roof for shelter. As they had to spend the night there in order to continue negotiations first thing in the morning, they found a spot to camp in a house occupied by the Red Army. Wia was worried. He knew that the soldiers could get so drunk that they would lose all control, and the presence of three young, foreign women might only fuel their lust. Fear of rape was not ungrounded—Claire, Mistou, and Plumette knew this very well. They obeyed Wia's instructions: he put them in a room where they all would sleep together, without removing their uniforms. He told them to push all the pieces of major furniture up against the door for better protection, should there be any attempts at nocturnal intrusion. He himself would remain within shouting distance. Two minutes later, he was back again. "I have a present for you," he said to Claire. Claire, full of anticipation, held out her hand and wondered what he could have possibly found in this place of ruin and desolation. "My dagger. Use it, if one of those drunkards manages in spite of everything to force open the door in hopes of raping you." And when he saw her astonished look: "Above all, don't hesitate to stab him in the throat or the heart." Then he went away. "Have you ever seen such a present?" joked Mistou. "Let's hope you won't have to use it," added Plumette. As for Claire, she stood staring at the dagger, fascinated. "My first present from Wia . . . " She knew already that there would be more.

And she was not mistaken. Wia has gotten into the habit of giving her presents, depending on what he manages to swap with the Brits or the Americans. Claire collects military badges that she sews inside the jacket of her uniform. The badges keep coming, but her dream is to have a Soviet red star. "It will be tricky, but I'll manage somehow. Just be patient, trust me," Wia promises. And with the childlike self-confidence that is entirely his own, "You hadn't noticed? I'm very resourceful!"

Is his confidence justified, or is he boasting? Claire cannot figure the man out. He's not like anyone she's ever known, he surprises her, amuses her, frightens her. There are times she finds him very handsome, and other times he's just too bizarre— immensely tall, as thin as a survivor, with deep blue eyes—and those protruding ears. He has a certain charm, of that she is sure: every time he shows up she has further proof of it. The moment Wia enters a room, the girls become more flirtatious and the men revert to manly camaraderie. No matter what the circumstances, Wia puts everyone in a good mood, men and women alike. He never seems to realize the effect he has on people. Claire in particular is disconcerted by his candor. And what if he's simply an idiot, an uneducated idiot?

"Dear Lord, Mistou, what is going to become of me? What is happening to me?"

Mistou, who is awake now and resigned to the fact, reaches for a pack of cigarettes, lights two and hands one to Claire.

"Is it your admirer who's gotten you into such a state?"

Claire is startled, indignant. Wia has been equally polite and charming with all the women in the building, no matter their age or position, but very soon it became apparent that there was one woman in particular who interested him. The Red Cross girls and the secretaries of the Displaced Persons Section alike very quickly realized that there was one of them who filled him with admiration and emotion.

"What admirer? What are you talking about? I don't understand."

"The Russian prince with the huge ears that stick out."

"That's the best thing about him, his huge sticking-out ears!"

Claire is sincere. She was about to confide in Mistou, confess her terror at the thought that she might be in love, her joy, too, but a sudden pain prevents her. She stubs out her cigarette and collapses on the pillow with a moan.

"I can feel it, here it comes, it's getting stronger . . . "

"What is?"

"My migraine."

As she left the room to join the others Mistou carefully pulled the curtains so the daylight would not disturb her friend. Claire was moaning miserably, but Mistou could not help but call from the doorway, "Which has a worse effect on you? The Russian prince or a migraine?" Her laughter in the stairway brought Claire to the verge of tears. She doesn't want to get up or see her friends or have to meet Wia's questioning gaze. How could she have let herself go to such a strong impulse? After she broke up with Patrice, she swore she would go no further than a few flings: that was the price to pay to preserve her precious hard-won liberty. And now here she is falling in love with a foreigner about whom she knows nothing, a former Russian, practically a Soviet, who has no profession and is from a milieu not her own, "a cosmopolitan milieu," or so people say. To fall in love with a man, any man, is a risk. And to fall in love with one like him . . . Claire has always managed to avoid suffering. She is very good at keeping her admirers at a distance, at using irony, making fun of them, discouraging them. Always with a mixture of humor and friendliness which means they cannot hold it against her. She thinks that she doesn't amount to much, yet, and if a man falls in love with her he's being rather naïve. A naïve man who is mistaken, where she is concerned. If she is honest, this is exactly what she felt about Patrice, as well as about André, and the young lieutenant in Béziers whose name she has forgotten, and Pierrot, and Minko. Correction: no, Minko does not belong on this list. She had immediately sensed the danger, and the power of his charm. After the business with the ambulance she found ways to avoid him, and her instinct provided marvelous protection. So why hasn't it done its job here in Berlin?

Berlin, from the moment it was carved up in July, 1945, has become a gigantic machine for sorting refugees. Roughly half a million arrive each month in the British and American sectors. Germans, mostly women, children, and old people; people expelled from Czechoslovakia; prisoners of war and anyone at all fleeing the Soviets. Initial figures predict that during the winter 1945-1946 almost twenty million Germans, over a quarter of the population, will be on the move in the ruined country. This enormous influx of ravaged survivors is complicating the work of Léon de Rosen's section and the French and Belgian Red Cross. There has been no letup for the residents of 96 Kurfürstendamm: they go to the train stations, the Soviet camps, and even farther afield, the moment anyone notifies them of a possible French presence. In Frankfurt-an-der-Oder there are trains disgorging people who no longer have a nationality, or identity, or place in the world. Among them there are Jews who have miraculously survived, Germans who fled Hitler's regime, and Frenchmen who had volunteered to serve in the Wehrmacht and who are trying to pass themselves off as former prisoners, Alsatians, or *malgré-nous*. All of them, as soon as they disembark, are transferred to the Zehlendorf displaced-persons camp, which is entirely under the control of the Americans. By November, 1945, there are an estimated five thousand people or more in this camp alone, of thirteen different nationalities. Fifty or more additional transit camps have been hastily set up around Berlin.

Every day Claire witnesses the tragic fate of these thousands of human beings. To be able to rescue even a few of them is like an answer to her own questions, a justification for her existence. This no longer has much to do with what she knew during the war, in Béziers. She's no longer being called on to take part in heroic deeds, or support the Résistance; she is no longer expected to follow the armies of liberation, but rather to join a battle that is far more obscure and thankless to rescue people from oblivion and death. She knows now how deeply she loves her life in Berlin. It is a cruel and sordid life, yet strangely beautiful at the same time—not unlike the ruined city itself, which is being rebuilt willy-nilly. It is like during the war, when she was surprised to find herself leading a life she thought was reserved for the heroines in novels, the novels she devoured as an adolescent, and which always made her own daily life seem so drab.

"Where does Wia belong in all this?" she wonders, as she finishes brushing her teeth. Her migraine is gone, and a few hours of sleep have left her feeling rested. She is no more serene for all that, but her sense of responsibility has regained the upper hand: she must go and find Plumette and ask her what the program for the day is, and what her own priorities are.

Mistou has left for a few days of rest in Paris. Claire gave her some letters for her family, and photographs, studio portraits taken in a very flattering lighting: she thinks she looks pretty for once. "A regular movie star!" said one of the girls. "Even your uniform looks as if it had been borrowed, and your cross of Lorraine looks as if it were made of diamonds! Who could ever imagine the dog's life you're leading here," said another. "Claire looks really great and we girls are proud of her," concluded Rolanne.

For two solid days, trains have been bringing in the Alsatians. Claire and Wia go together to meet them. For once, the Soviets haven't tried to hide any of them, and some of the officers whom Wia has befriended have actually made things easier. Claire has no time to wonder about their mutual feelings, but she has noticed a certain change in Wia's behavior toward her. He is even more attentive, in a better mood than ever and—something that is quite unlike him—extraordinarily discreet. Contrary to what she might have feared, he has made no allusion to any sort of fond feelings, nor has he ever tried to see her alone. But she knows that he is constantly looking at her. A curiously confident look, as if he knows what the future has in store for them and is giving her the time to find out for herself.

On the evening of November 11 they throw a big party at 96 Kurfürstendamm to celebrate the 1918 armistice. Every floor is open, and the front door stays open all the time, with a constant flow of guests joining the usual tenants. French, British, Americans, and Soviets all getting along perfectly, forgetting for a few hours everything that divides them during the day. As there is a far greater number of men than women, the girls from the French and Belgian Red Cross are in constant demand on the dance floor, whirling from one pair of arms to the next. The French-women are wearing their regulation "RAF blue" uniforms, but they have all taken the time to put on makeup and do their hair.

"You look really lovely," murmurs Wia into Claire's ear. He is holding her close, and he says the same thing over and over, relentlessly. She has granted him several dances in a row and is paying no attention to any of the other officers. In the beginning they seemed annoyed, but now they've given up on her and word has gone around to leave her alone. If she were at all attentive she would have noticed that nobody is bothering them: it is as though they're completely on their own.

Claire is attentive only to what she is feeling for Wia, the sense of security he gives her, which is something completely new. He is not a good dancer, and he frequently steps on her toes, and he does not say anything to her other than his standard, "You look really lovely," which in the long run makes him seem a bit ridiculous. He doesn't know how to converse, thinks

Claire. And far from being alarming, this discovery amuses her. When she is in his arms, it is like with no other man she has known. She feels herself becoming a woman again, and the sudden intensity of it is unsettling. With an involuntary reflex of self-defense, she makes as if to push him away: "It's unbelievable how badly you dance!" she says.

"Unbelievable?"

"Yes."

"Is that serious?" Far from being annoyed, he laughs.

"Yes. Well, no . . . " He holds her head in his hand and guides it gently toward his chest until Claire feels the rough cloth of his military jacket against her cheek. He has closed his arms around her shoulders and is holding her very close. She can hear his breathing, calm and regular, and the murmur of his voice near her ear. "What are you mumbling about?" "I'm not mumbling, I'm speaking to you in Russian." They stay there silently for a few minutes, hardly moving, while all around them the other dancers are going wild to the rhythm of a boogie-woogie. Finally he steps back, holding her at arm's length, and he looks her straight in the eyes with a curious mixture of intense joy and gravity: "I love you. Yes that's exactly what it is, I love you and I do not want to live without you."

Mistou is back from Paris. She has brought some letters, warm clothes, and the first issue of a new woman's magazine, *Elle.* On the cover a beautiful woman in a red jacket and a black hat is smiling as she holds up a ginger cat with green eyes. Mistou has just come into the kitchen where Claire, Rolanne, and the two drivers from the Belgian Red Cross are warming up with a cup of tea. They are about to leave on a mission. A delicate mission that they are dreading: their job will be to take the children known to have French fathers from their German mothers. Most of the men were forcibly enrolled in the STO, the Compulsory Work Service.

"Listen to this, girls," says Mistou, sitting on the table.

She opens the newspaper to page 3 and reads, "'We haven't seen them for five years. Time has gone by and the little girls have grown up. Jules Raimu has a twenty-year-old daughter, Paulette . . . Etc., etc., etc. Claire Mauriac, daughter of the author of *Les Mal-Aimés,* is presently in Berlin. As an ambulance driver for the Red Cross, she is in charge of repatriating the last French prisoners left in the Russian zone. She hasn't had time yet to think about what she will do later on.' You're famous, Clarinette, famous!"

Mistou hands the magazine to her friend. Claire looks silently at the portraits of the five young women: her presence among these strangers immediately makes her feel embarrassed and disheartened. Until she read this article she thought she had obtained what she wanted so badly when she joined the Red Cross: to become an integral member of a group. She tried very hard to succeed, to think and say "we" rather than "I." By choosing her rather than Rolanne or Plumette, the magazine has once again made her into what she was before the war: "The daughter of . . . "

The kitchen door opens and Wia comes in noisily with a carton of American cigarettes in his hand.

"Here you are, girls. And for you, dear Claire . . . "

He has something in his closed fist, and he waves it in front of her face, laughing with delight.

"What is it?"

"Guess . . . "

He makes the game last, thrilled to be the center of attention of the five young women. Claire shoves the magazine to one side, the better to respond to his request: "Animal, vegetable, or mineral?" Wia is having fun, and they all share his mood except for Mistou, who is beginning to understand that something has changed in the atmosphere in the apartment.

Wia feels at home here, and Claire is beaming with a childish joy that Mistou has never seen.

"Hey, you two . . . "

But no one is paying any attention to her. The girls surround Wia and beg him to open his fist and show them what he's hiding.

"Instead of the ring I can't offer you just yet . . . "

It's a military badge with a red star, and it goes from hand to hand while Wia tells them how he got it during a drinking bout with the Soviet officers. As usual, he takes the starring role, assigning his fictional self qualities he doesn't have in order to enhance his story, but he is having such a good time that no one would dream of reproaching him. Claire is delighted, the Soviet badge has become the jewel in her collection, and that very evening she will get someone to sew it for her to the inside of the jacket of her uniform.

"Can you do it for me, Rolanne dear? You know how bad I am at sewing . . . "

Wia sees the magazine, still open on the table, and grabs hold of it, curious. Claire's photograph elicits a whistle of admiration.

"'Author of *Les Mal-Aimés* . . . ' He's a writer? He's your father?"

Because Claire is hesitant to reply, both shocked by his ignorance and flattered by the role reversal that makes François Mauriac merely "the father of . . . ," Wia hurries on. "The article isn't only about you, Claire, it's about all of you girls. It's great that they're acknowledging the fantastic work you're doing in Berlin."

He lowers his voice and places a quick kiss on her fingers: "I'm proud of you."

Claire looks down to hide her emotion. What a gift he has for always seeing the good side of things. Life with him is becoming mysteriously simple.

Mistou had forgotten to give Claire the letter Claire's

mother had brought to her a few hours before she was due to leave Paris. Only at the end of the evening, after a long day spent with the German women, did the letter reach Claire. It was a reply to the note in which she'd hastily told her family about meeting Wia. She'd been carried away by her need to talk about him, and had hidden neither his Russian origins nor his uncertainty about the future, after Berlin. And now she is sorry she shared all of that. As she might have suspected, her mother is concerned, full of warnings against this stranger; she wants to know more about his family and their standard of living. Her mother is insinuating that Claire is losing her head in Berlin: she must take herself in hand and come back to Paris for good. The only explanation she can find for what she considers to be "an absurd infatuation" is medical: Claire is overworked, and that is yet another reason to return to France so they can look after her. Claire's mother reminds her that the war is over, and that her place, her only true place, is at 38 Avenue Théophile-Gautier, with her family.

Claire puts down the letter, disheartened. Her mother is treating her like a little girl, showing her the path she must take—worse than that, giving her orders. Once again they have failed to realize she has become a woman. She knows that behind her mother is her father, her sister and her brothers, and that all of them are in agreement regarding her future. At the same time, because she loves them, she is sorry to give them cause for concern. She has just had the most trying day, and her mood is already bleak. On two occasions, she and Rolanne had to take a baby away from a German mother. It was an order. The French fathers had been reported missing, and yet the children were to be taken from their mothers and repatriated to France where, perhaps, no one would want them.

"You think too much, Clarinette, come to sleep."

In the big bed, Mistou yawns and stretches. She hasn't finished unpacking her things, and her open suitcase is lying in the middle of the room, her clothes scattered here and there. Claire feels suddenly comforted to have her friend by her side again, with her inevitable mess and carefree attitude. Yes, with Mistou back, the floozies' room will be filled with life again. Claire is tired, she'll follow Mistou to bed, and sleep. She'll reply to her mother's letter tomorrow.

> November 28
> My dear Mama,
> I just found out we'll be leaving in ten minutes. It's eight o'clock in the morning and we're going to the funeral of three Alsatians who did not survive their transfer.
> I got your letter last night. Don't worry, I'm very happy.
> I'll write you a longer letter later today or tomorrow, but I wanted to reassure you this morning.
> We're going to Paris on the twelfth.
> Very big hug and lots of kisses.

She signs the letter. But before slipping it into the envelope she underlines the most important thing, pressing hard: *I'm very happy*.

For four days, Claire shuts herself away in a dark silence that surprises everyone. Naturally they ask her what is wrong, but she replies evasively, pleading a migraine. She seems nervous, irritable, very different from the young woman beloved by all in the building. Wia is the most worried, questioning her endlessly, insisting, imploring, and even provoking her. The second evening, in the kitchen on the first floor, he gets carried away and makes a scene in the presence of the girls. Claire immediately rushes to her room. Wia wants to follow her but Rolanne stops him, grabbing him by the sleeve. "Please, just leave her alone," she says gently. Wia glares at her, then leaves the kitchen, slamming the door so violently that they all jump. The next morning he too is silent, with a hangdog look that ought to have made them laugh, but it merely makes them feel sorry for him. He goes up and down the stairway for no reason, in the hopes of running into Claire. But she hardly goes out, or if she does, it is on a mission where his presence is not required. For fear of being rebuffed by her companions, he has stopped going to see them. And besides, Plumette and Rolanne seem to be avoiding him. Only Mistou, when he runs into her, favors him with a brilliant smile and a carefree "Don't look so upset, it will all work out."

On the evening of the fourth day, Mistou goes up to find Wia.

"Claire has just gone out on her own somewhere. If you want to talk to her, now's your chance . . . but don't tell her that I'm the one who told you . . . "

Wia grabs his coat and hurries down the stairs.

It is dark outside, and an icy wind is driving the half-melted snow along the ground. The street is deserted, and before long he spots the long military coat, shapka, and fur-lined boots. Claire is walking very quickly. He wants to call out to her but then thinks better of it and stifles an oath. What is she doing alone outside? Where is she going? Berlin is an extremely dangerous city, women know this and never go out on their own. Wia thinks that Claire must be on her way to a tryst. The physical pain of it takes his breath away. He knows that she is brave and courageous—is she not in the habit of saying, "I love danger"? She must have an appointment with someone, a man, of course, that's why she's been avoiding him for four days. He moans with pain at the thought that she might be mocking him, betraying him.

Claire abruptly leaves Kurfürstendamm and turns right. Wia is filled with a cold rage. He's going to follow them, surprise them, confront them. He sets off on her trail, careful to hug the walls so that he won't be caught if she turns around.

It's a needless precaution: the narrow street is plunged in total darkness. There is no light at all from the ruined buildings, not a trace of any human presence. But Wia knows that hundreds of Berliners continue to live buried in their cellars.

Claire stops and seems to hesitate. Then she knocks on a door cobbled together with planks and pieces of cardboard. The door opens at once and she disappears inside. Wia is completely taken aback. A romantic tryst in such a place is out of the question. What is she up to? He decides not to prolong the unbearable mystery another second, and follows her into the ruins.

Then suddenly Claire comes out again. They bump into each other, she slips, tries to grab his coat, slips again, loses her balance and falls onto the ground, onto the wet snow that is beginning to freeze.

"Wia, oh, Wia!"

Contrary to what he expects, she bursts out laughing. A nervous, joyful, painful laugh, and he stares at her speechless, petrified, with the sensation that nothing he sees is real, that soon he will wake up and leave this nightmare behind.

"Help me up, we can't stay here," she says between two hiccups. "Oh, Wia, it's so good to see you, so good!"

He holds her close to him as they head back the way they have come. They are both struggling against the wind, which hinders their attempts at an explanation. But Wia has grasped the gist of it, the reason why Claire came to this narrow street in the ruins. Once she has sworn him to secrecy, her story is stupefying. On her own initiative, without telling a soul, Claire went to warn a young German woman that her baby would be taken away from her the next day. Claire is defiant, provocative, as she swears to Wia that she doesn't give a damn about martial law; she is convinced that justice, the most elementary form of justice, is on her side. She describes how these unmarried German mothers have suffered—no roof, or heat, virtually nothing to eat, nothing left but a child. Claire is adamant: in this instance, the policy of the Red Cross and the Section of Displaced Persons is both cruel and barbaric. Wia knows how devoted she is to both these organizations, and that she has always agreed with all their ideas, all their moral principles. Now she is being careless to the point of irresponsibility, but he cannot help but admire the strength of her convictions, her physical pluck, her courage. "You've got some nerve," he murmurs as they enter their building. And without giving her the time to reply, he says earnestly, "I think I understand you." Claire is not sure, but she can see the effort he is making to be closer to her.

In the stairs they meet Mistou: her face lights up.

"Well, friends again?"

"Yes."

"And . . . in love?"

"Yes."

Wia takes Claire by her shoulders, holds her against him and says defiantly, as if to the whole world, "Yes, Mistou, in love, very much in love. For always."

Mistou is already asleep when Claire goes into the bedroom. Without making a sound she removes her jacket and her little boots and switches on the night light. The warmth of the room seems perfect to her, and the silence helps her clarify her thoughts. She is ready, now, to write to her parents.

> December 4, 1945
> My dear Mama, my dear Papa,
> A plane is leaving tomorrow morning, and a friend will deliver this letter to you in the early afternoon.
> Forgive me for taking so long to write, but I have just had four dreadful days. I didn't know what I wanted, and I think I no longer knew who I was. But no doubt it was something I had to go through.
> What I have to tell you is of the greatest importance because my happiness, and my life, are at stake.
> Wia loves me and I love him.
> He loves going out in the evening and I hate it; he loves to see friends and I hate it; he loves to drink and I hate it; he loves to tell funny stories and I hate it; we have absolutely nothing in common, but I think that it just might be with him that I have a chance at happiness.
> I am asking for your consent to marry him, and please send me your answer as quickly as possible.
> As planned I will be in Paris on the twelfth and Wia hopes to get a twenty-four hour leave to come and meet you.
> Dear Mama, dear Papa, I kiss you tenderly.
> Your little Claire
>
> PS: I'm not sure I'll make a very presentable princess.

C laire and Wia run down the stairs to the girls' apartment on the first floor. They have all been waiting
impatiently to hear how it went: Claire has called her
mother in Paris. But from the way Claire and Wia burst into
the kitchen they understand immediately: they surround them
with hugs and shouts of joy, applause and questions. When
everyone has calmed down, Wia proposes a toast to their
future wedding and disappears to hunt for a hypothetical bottle of champagne. Rolanne heats up some coffee, and they all
settle around the table.

Claire suddenly feels exhausted, so weary that she cannot
reply to her friends' questions in any detail. It must be the after-
effect of these hours of tension, the shock of hearing her
mother's voice on the telephone. It was the first time she had
used the one telephone line to France that had been set up in
the office of the Displaced Persons Section; Léon de Rosen
arranged for her to make the call. Claire had waited feverishly,
with an anxiety that has not yet completely left her. But it
would seem her parents have given her their consent, and she
is going to marry Wia . . . A sudden rush of doubt, and her heart
sinks. What if, as with Patrice, she is making a mistake? What
if, yet again, she has become a victim of someone's love for
her—victim of his enthusiasm, his certainty that they are made
for each other?

"What's wrong, my little Clarinette? You're all pale," says
Rolanne worriedly.

"Are you getting a migraine?" says Mistou sarcastically, lifting her hands to her temples and giving a perfect imitation of Claire's grimacing and the plaintive intonation of her voice: "'It's there, I can feel it, it's getting stronger, oh, no, ouch . . .'"

"That's not funny, making fun of her. If you had ever even once in your life had a migraine headache, you would know that it's horribly painful."

"Oh, if we can't even make a joke anymore . . . "

Claire is cheered somewhat by the sight of her friends arguing over her. She gets up and goes to the window. It is dark outside and the snow lies heavy over the city. She feels the warmth of the kitchen, compared to the temperature outside. She thinks about the men her team has saved and who will be sleeping in a bed for the first time in so long. And her thoughts return fleetingly, involuntarily, to her friends who have died during the war. But I am alive. This awareness of life is so intense that she whirls around to confront her friends' worried faces; they had fallen silent when she turned her back on them.

"Do you have any idea just what is at stake in a marriage between a French girl from a good family and a Russian ex-prince who lost his entire fortune because of a revolution?"

Wia is standing motionless at the entrance to the kitchen, in the darkness of the doorway. No one heard him come into the apartment, and he is gazing with curiosity at the young women, their cheerful faces as they listen to Claire. She is giving them her own, very comical, rendition of the telephone call that he listened in on. Already as an actual witness he had failed to grasp the better part of it, but now, because of her clowning mimicry, he no longer understands a thing.

"So, Papa is a bit wary. In Paris, all the Russians are taxi drivers or musicians in nightclubs, whether they are princes or not. 'What are we going to do, what are we going to do?' wails Mama when she rereads my letter for the umpteenth time. Papa has an idea: 'Let's call Troyat!' Troyat, Henri Troyat, is a great friend of my older brother Claude. He's a Russian immigrant like Wia, an exile like Wia, a naturalized Frenchman, again, just like Wia. The only difference is that he has taken a pseudonym and he's a writer. He even got the Prix Goncourt in 1938 with a book called *L'Araigne* and let me tell you, he threw one hell of a party that day . . . "

"A first instance of closer Franco-Russian ties," says Rolanne dreamily.

"Precisely . . . So, Papa calls Troyat and puts him in charge of finding out more about this so-called prince with the name of Yvan Wiazemsky. Troyat can tell he's really worried, and tries to reassure him: 'The name rings a bell, nothing unseemly, of course . . . I'll call you back.' Papa goes to join Mama in the drawing room. They are so nervous that all they can do is wait. Mama, as always, is expecting the worst, something at which she's a real champion. Papa gets annoyed: 'Do be quiet, Jeanne, for the love of God, hush!' I can just hear them. Ring, ring! They dash to the telephone, Papa picks up and he can hear Troyat, bursting with enthusiasm, delighted: 'Not only is Wiazemsky not bad at all, it's downright excellent! You cannot do better!' And he goes on to tell Papa that Yvan comes from one of the oldest families in Russia, they go all the way back to the year 800 or something. Papa is still a little bit wary: 'Are you sure he's not a crook?' Troyat is having a ball. 'Of course I'm sure. Before the war, he lived with his sister and parents not far from where you are, on the rue Raynouard. His parents are still there, and it could be you actually pass each other in the street on a regular basis.' My parents are relieved, Mama calls me and gives me their consent to marry Wia. Papa picks up the receiver and—referring to the PS in my letter—cannot help but say, 'If you want to become a presentable princess, you'd better get started on it right away!' That's it, end of story!"

"Bravo, what a show!"

Wia strides into the kitchen, applauding wildly. The neck of a bottle is sticking out of one pocket of his military greatcoat; in the other pocket, grossly distended, something is wiggling, but no one notices. Claire continues acting the clown, bidding farewell to her audience. Wia sets the champagne bottle down on the table, and the girls bring glasses. He pours each of them a glass, then turns to Claire: "Am I mistaken, or do we owe our engagement to an ex-Russian—although his name is unfamiliar to me. How do we know he's a real Russian? Maybe he's the crook your father is so afraid of . . . "

"Oh, Wia, don't go mixing things up! The investigation was about you, not him. I can't believe you haven't heard of this young Russian who was naturalized and won the Prix Goncourt. You may not know anything about literature, granted, but surely you've heard about him through the Russian community! You must have all been very proud, and celebrated the event!"

Creasing his forehead with effort, Wia tries to remember. He wants to please Claire, or at least not disappoint her, and what she's been telling him about the young writer is slowly beginning to sound familiar. But it's not what she thinks.

"If your writer is the Russian I'm thinking about, one of the Tarassof sons, our community, as you call it, did not all celebrate. Many of them were hurt by the fact he changed his name when he became French. My sister Nina was shocked, and she's quite angry with him."

He spoke slowly, an unusual sadness settling over his features. Claire suddenly realizes that Wia has never yet spoken to her about his family, or about the Russian community he grew up in. He's hardly even mentioned his parents and his sister—whose name she has just heard for the first time: Nina. Until this point, they were caught up in trying to obtain the consent of Claire's family, not Wia's. Naturally they only recently decided to marry, and they have been so busy with work. But still, thinks Claire, we really hardly know each other . . .

A strange sound, part moan, part whimper, distracts her from her thoughts. As if by magic, Wia is once again full of cheer. He thrusts his hand into the pocket of his greatcoat and removes a large ball of fur and sets it down in the middle of the table among the champagne glasses and the ashtrays full of cigarette butts: a puppy, scarcely three months old, now staring terrified at the people leaning over him.

"I nearly forgot the most important thing of all. Before we even get married, there are three of us, my sweet. A kid in the street sold him to me. He claims he's a pure schnauzer, but I haven't been able to find out for sure. Apparently schnauzers were stable dogs originally, because they get along well with horses. So when I teach you to ride horseback, he'll be able to come with us."

In spite of the cold and snow, Claire and Wia go for a walk in what was once a park and now is nothing but a scattered collection of trees, earth, and roots. This wartime landscape strengthens their desire to live each day to the fullest, their determination to start something together. The puppy trots ahead of them. From time to time Claire lets go of Wia's arm and picks up a piece of wood or a pine cone and tosses it ahead of her. Or she runs until she's out of breath, the puppy hot on her heels.

Wia gazes after her. He loves her slim figure tightly belted in her navy blue Red Cross coat, her round, pink, childlike cheeks, her thick brown hair escaping from the shapka. And he thinks she is the most precious thing in the world, and that she will be leaving for Paris in two days. He trusts her, trusts who they are together, and what he calls a bit pompously "their destiny." But he is also a very superstitious man, and he cannot help but knock on wood; in his pocket he always keeps a jade miniature as a good-luck charm.

December 5, 1945
Dear Mama,

Please don't be cross with me for not having found the time to tell you how happy I am, but you have to understand that I'm no longer eighteen years old, and the thought of getting married is no longer enough to make me completely lose my head. I'm very happy, I'm completely sure of that, but it's not the only thing I think about in the course of a day.

There's all the rest of life, all the horrible suffering of mankind, the terrible times we are living in, and above all the certainty of death. In the midst of all this, a wedding can only be a happy event, but it may also be the prelude to very very sad things, because why should I be eternally happy in the end, why should I be spared the suffering that is the lot of everyone around me?

Forgive me, Mama dear, because I know this must not sound particularly cheery. It must be because of the morning, which was cold and dreary.

Do you know the Mr. Rose who writes, I think, for *Le Monde*?

He spent several months in a camp, and he lost his wife, his son, and I think his daughter. He came here to fetch the body of his son who died in Ravensbrück. Rolanne drove the ambulance yesterday on this sad mission with him.

This morning we attended a brief ceremony. I often found myself looking over at the father. The sight was unbearable. I was trembling with cold and sadness, thinking about him, about his family who had been massacred, and about all the people who have shared his fate. When you witness so much injustice, how can you think about being happy? Do I even have that right?

It will do me a lot of good to see you again, and see Paris. I deeply love my life here in Berlin, but there are times when it is just too painful. I am longing to leave, I'm fed up, and I'm tired.

Sending you many tender kisses.

In Paris, Claire spends time with friends and wanders through the city in search of buried memories. The Occupation still seems very recent, and at times she is surprised not to see the gray-green uniforms anymore, here and there along the avenues. She finds it hard to make any connection between the erstwhile conquerors and the thousands of vanquished survivors in Germany, in Berlin. When she talks about it to her friends, she can hardly arouse anything more than polite attention. They are more interested in her stories about her companions in the Red Cross and her upcoming marriage to Wia. She shows them photographs, tries to describe their work. She refrains from telling them how little interest life in Paris holds for her now. That was not the case initially, when the joy of seeing her family was greater than anything. But very quickly her parents, her brothers, and her sister went back to their usual routine and Claire began to feel isolated, as on every visit, as if she had no real connection to life at 38 Avenue Théophile-Gautier.

Every day she gets a long letter from Wia bringing her up to date on the slightest details of life in Berlin. He too likes to write, and Claire discovers that he is totally at ease with the French language. For the first time he talks to her about his family—how they left the Crimea in April, 1919, and journeyed to Malta and then on to London. But in each of his letters he insists that he is French and would rather not be part of the Russian community: he feels no nostalgia whatsoever about the past.

At last she receives the news she has been so eagerly await-
ing: Wia will be there on December 31 in the morning, and in
the evening he will go to join his parents and his sister Nina in
Compiègne, where they are staying for the time being. Claire
won't be able to meet them this time, and she must confess she
is relieved: these introductions between their two families are
trying obligations she would rather live without. Fortunately
Wia feels exactly the same way: "The ordeal I'll have to go
through at your house is more than enough for the time
being," he says during one of their rare telephone conversations. Claire is surprised, once again, to see how trusting he is.
He seems to be convinced he will be well received. He cannot
understand why Claire worries about his first encounter with
the people he already refers to as "my future in-laws." So much
so that he scolds her: "Why do you always have to complicate
everything?" She agrees, then warns him, "But you'll see, when
you live with me it will be worse, because we'll be together all
the time." What is merely a mild prediction sounds like a
threat: just one of Claire's ways of being provocative with others, but it can baffle the people around her. She knows it, and
sometimes goes on to regret it, but she can't help doing exactly
the same thing whenever the opportunity arises. This time,
however, Wia's long sorrowful silence on the telephone is dis-
quieting, and she realizes how much more easily she can hurt
him than any of her previous admirers. She reminds herself
that he is in Berlin and she is in Paris, and it would not take
much for some sort of misunderstanding to arise. She suddenly
fears it could even cause them to break up, and the thought is
so violently painful that the very sound of her voice is altered.
"I'm joking. Come quickly, Yvan, come quickly." She very
rarely calls him by his first name and he instantly forgets her
unsettling words. But there is something else he wants to make
perfectly clear: "Since I became French, I no longer call myself
Yvan, but Jean. I'm sure your parents will appreciate my pride

in being French. It's important, don't forget it when you talk to them about me."

But Wia is mistaken.

Claire's family, without exception, adore his exotic Russian first name and have no intention of giving it up. They are delighted with the young man's open, straightforward personality, and they are prepared to give him their trust and Claire's hand in marriage. Everything would be going perfectly had it not been for a sudden death in the family: Claire's uncle, her father's brother, the abbot Jean, died in mysterious circumstances, that have yet to be elucidated. Claire can see how upset her parents are, her father in particular; he is making a great effort to hide his sorrow and provide a warm welcome to the newcomer. Under less tragic circumstances, she knows he would have been more attentive and would have plied Wia with questions about his plans for the future, his tastes, his religion. She knows, too, that he would have asked to meet Wia's family in order to get a more complete picture of his future son-in-law.

She tries to explain this to Wia, who refuses to take it into account. For him the meeting has been a success, because he has obtained permission to marry Claire without any prior conditions. They have two more hours to spend together before he takes the train for Compiègne, so they decide to go for a walk through the Latin Quarter.

It's very cold, snow is forecast, and they walk up and down the lanes in the Luxembourg Gardens, holding each other, in love. To their delight and amusement they see other couples just like them. Claire has set aside her fears, the unpleasant sensation that her parents did not really understand who Wia is, that they might withdraw their hastily granted consent. The sheer physical bliss of being in his arms is extraordinarily intense, and with it comes the certainty that despite all the differences between them she will be happy at his side. The garden is so beautiful in the December mist, yet she feels strangely detached from her surroundings.

"Where are we going to have the wedding?" she asks suddenly.

"Wherever you want."

"In Berlin. Our life is there. Our real life . . . "

"But our parents are not exactly young anymore, and it would be horribly uncomfortable for them in Berlin, don't you think?"

"But all our friends are in Berlin."

They walk on in silence for a moment. Wia points to a statue.

"When we were children, my mother used to bring my sister and me to play in the Luxembourg Garden. She always arranged to meet the other Russian mothers by the statue of one of the queens of France. I know them all by heart: Marguerite de Valois . . . "

But Claire is no longer listening, she is lost in her own childhood memory of the mysterious sadness inside that she grew up with and which has never really left. A sadness that would fade somewhat during the summer vacations in Gironde or in the Landes, but that always returned as soon as it was time to start school again in Paris. Suddenly she hears herself saying, "When we finish our work in Berlin, I don't think I want to come back to Paris to live . . . "

"Where, then?"

"I don't know. In a foreign country. Far away."

Claire knows that if anyone can grant her this wish to be elsewhere, it is Wia. And what if that is why she has chosen him?

Almost two months have gone by since the day they said goodbye at the Gare du Nord. To Claire the time has seemed endless, despite her family, and the time spent with her friends, with Martine her co-worker from Béziers, who now has a little boy. She has been to the theater, on her own or with friends, to see premieres of plays by authors, all of them new to her: *Les Bouches inutiles,* by Simone de Beauvoir, *Caligula* by Albert Camus, and the restaging of Jean Cocteau's *Les Parents terribles.* And there is a film that enchanted her—she's been to see it three times, and dreams of taking Wia to see it: *Les Enfants du Paradis.* She has been listening to music, and shopping for gifts to take back to her Red Cross companions.

Claire hums to herself as she finishes packing. That morning she went to the hairdresser's, and she's had a manicure. She wants to look beautiful for Wia—she'll see him again at the end of the day if the plane for Berlin leaves on time. In the meanwhile she'll have lunch one last time with the entire family—her parents, her brothers, and her sister with her husband and two little girls.

Claire takes her "RAF blue" uniform from the wardrobe and puts it on. She likes the straight skirt and the long close-fitting jacket with its shining cross of Lorraine. Claire knows that leaving her civilian clothing behind will restore a certain self-confidence and sense of legitimacy. She's eager to get back to work as an ambulance driver, eager to be back at 96 Kurfürstendamm.

As she is straightening up the room that will be her young girl's bedroom for only a short while longer, she comes across the photo album from the vacations she spent in Montgenèvre in 1938 and 1939. She turns the pages slowly, allowing memories to surface. What interests her most is the spring of 1938: she was staying with her sister at the little La Chaumière hotel, and this was their first vacation without their parents, and with everything that implied, including the heady discovery of freedom. In no time at all they had made a lot of friends and become the most popular girls at the resort. Everyone was fighting for time with the "delightful little Mauriac girls," as they were known.

Claire lingers in particular over a photograph of the two of them on the balcony of the wooden chalet, a range of snow-covered mountains in the background. They are both wearing short-sleeved blouses, visibly in the process of getting a suntan. Luce has her eyes closed and is smiling with pleasure. Claire has her eyes open wide, but looks dreamy, almost absent. What is she thinking about? Other photographs show the two sisters among the gang of friends that quickly formed and over whom they reigned like queens. Claire dwells for a long poignant moment over the pictures of one particular young man, hand-some and solid—Jock, always by her side. She remembers how they met, in a nightclub called Les Rois Mages: he was doing his military service. She remembers how they went skiing together, how happy they were to be together, how they met again in Paris and all the plans they made before they were separated by war. Claire remembers absolutely everything about Jock. Why on earth did she get engaged to Patrice? "Jock died, beheaded, in Cassino, in Italy," she thinks sorrowfully as she closes the photo album. "It's in the past," she says out loud. Eight years have gone by since she was that young girl in Montgenèvre, almost a lifetime. "It's in the past," she says again, still out loud. In the silence of her room, above her packed suitcases, her words resonate with a fierce determination.

A banner stretched across the stairway at 96 Kur-fürstendamm proclaims: "Welcome, Berlin's first fiancés." There is a loud burst of applause on every floor of the building when Wia appears, holding Claire by the hand. He is beaming with joy and pride, and he turns around with every step to gaze at her, as if he cannot get enough of her. She is more moved than she could ever have imagined when she sat dreaming in the airplane. Mistou and Rolanne hug her and tell her how happy they are to see her again, and Claire cannot hold back her tears. She finds refuge in Rolanne's arms, weeping like a child and saying over and over, "I am so happy, so happy . . . " But it's not long before Wia takes her from Rolanne's arms, and holding her by the waist he leads her up to the next floor where his team is waiting. A new round of applause, more hugging and kissing. Léon de Rosen embraces them one after the other and congratulates them. "You've made the right choice. We're all so proud of you. May God bless you." His serious demeanor, his stiff posture are too much for Claire, after her tears, and she bursts out laughing. "You're such a funny man, Rosen, you make me laugh . . . " The others begin to laugh, without really understanding what she meant, but her laughter is so infectious they can't help it, and soon it can be heard throughout the building.

The party lasts well into the night.

The morning is already half over by the time Claire wakes

up. The schnauzer, fully grown now, is asleep at the foot of the bed. His name is Kitz, and Claire and Mistou are the ones who look after him. Suddenly the door opens, and Plumette comes in unannounced. She's very pale.

"Hurry, get some clothes on, Wia and Léon are here and they're waiting for you. It's urgent."

Claire throws on the woolen dressing gown she brought back from Paris and follows Plumette onto the landing. She barely has time to register how pale the two men look; there are tears streaming down Wia's unshaven cheeks.

"I've been dismissed from the Army," he says in a barely audible voice.

February 26, 1946

Dear Papa,

There's been a most terrible upset, this morning early: Rosen received an order from Meyer, Minister for German Affairs, to dismiss Wia. On three counts:

1. Illicit trafficking with the Germans during the war.
2. Illicit profiteering.
3. Membership in La Cagoule.[4]

You can imagine the state poor Wia is in, and me as well. Naturally Rosen has done everything in his power to get to the bottom of the matter.

I don't think I have to tell you that Wia was never involved in any trafficking with the Germans.

As for La Cagoule, he merely went to a few meetings and never did a thing. He was twenty years old at the time.

My dear Papa, I'm so sorry for this new trouble. I confess I'm rather upset and I hope you'll be able to help us.

All of this, obviously, is the fault of the Communists. Which doesn't bode well for the future . . .

What can you do? Do you know Meyer?

I wonder if you should talk about it with Bidault.[5] It's our future that is at stake.

This morning when I woke up, I was so happy—talk about a cold shower.

I beg you to do something. Unless, of course, you think it would be better for you just to stay put.

---

[4] French fascist-leaning and anti-communist group, active in the 1930s.
[5] French politician active in the Résistance.

Forgive me for this letter, but I'm writing as fast as I can. The letter has to leave in a few minutes.

Dear Papa, forgive me, but please think about us.

I nearly took the plane to come and talk to you in person, but Rosen would rather I stayed with Yvan, who will certainly have to go to Paris in a very short while.

If he has to leave Berlin, Rosen won't stay. But we hope that everything will work out.

Papa, it is so easy for me to imagine the effect my letter is going to have on you that I don't know what else to say other than to apologize, but poor little Yvan is as unhappy today as he was happy yesterday, as sad as he was adorable.

I send you all my love.

Wia follows with his own letter to Monsieur François Mauriac, of the Académie Française:

Berlin, February 26, 1946

Dear Sir,

I don't know what to say, what to write. The term "Sir" seems grotesque and old-fashioned. I cannot write the words that I actually feel, today less than ever.

Yesterday when I went to meet Claire, I wondered what I had done for Our Lord to make me so happy. This morning I feel like I've been buried beneath a layer of mud, and I wonder why one hand is taking away what the other one gave me. Claire appeared in my life, and then suddenly this wretched business, the very next day—it would look like a bad melodrama if it were not true, horribly true. Rosen is going to put up a fight, he's full of fire and enthusiasm, fortified by the strength of our friendship.

I already suspected I was unworthy of so much happiness, and today I realize how crazy I was to think of it for even an instant. If only the notice hadn't appeared in *Le Figaro*. Because of it, you too will be besmirched, at a time when more than ever you must be without reproach, the way a flag must be.

I'm surprised I can even remain lucid, but I am fully lucid when I remind you of the words of the Gospel: "And if thy hand offend thee, cut it off."

Claire and I love each other, and I know that this business

won't change any of that. But on a material level, on a vital level, it will upset everything, and it would be pointless to deny that. Don't be afraid, if it comes to that, of throwing me overboard, Claire agrees with me on this. I won't drown, and Claire's love will protect me.

If you can find out who is behind this, it will make it easier for me to defend myself and—as soon as I have the strength—to counterattack.

I've enclosed a declaration I wrote this morning all in one go, summing up my defense.

Please do not commit your name to the defense of a bad cause if what you find out shows you right from the start that my cause is a lost one.

If you take my defense in the presence of others, don't go on secretly condemning me, which would be even worse.

With all my love and respect, I beg for your forgiveness.

Yvan.

Declaration of Jean Wiazemsky:

I, the undersigned, Jean Wiazemsky, Lieutenant in the reserve, Croix de guerre 1939-1940, presently Secretary of the Displaced Persons Section of the French group of the Council of Control, do hereby declare, on my honor:

1. I have never been involved in any illicit trafficking with the Germans.

2. I have never made any illicit profit through trafficking with the Germans.

These two accusations against me are absolutely groundless. I am prepared to provide irrefutable proof by demonstrating that I was taken prisoner by the Germans at the Somme front on June 7, 1940, and then remained in captivity in Germany until April 21, 1945, when I was liberated by the Red Army.

As for my behavior during the five years of captivity, I will if necessary provide affidavits from individuals beyond reproach, not only French but also British and Soviet, given the fact that I was in a camp where all these nationalities were detained together.

I was liberated on April, 21, placed myself at the disposition of the Soviet command, and was subsequently in charge of an irregular force of partisans acting in liaison with the elements closest to the Red Army.

Pursuant to my conduct during the last weeks of the war my name was put forward for the Legion of Honor by the commanding physician, Dr. Meunier, who is presently surgeon at the Dominique-Larrey hospital in Versailles, and who at the time was chief physician at the hospital where I was located.

I was part of a prisoner exchange with the Americans on May 21, and after a month spent helping to organize displaced persons camps for French prisoners in the Russian zone, I was recruited directly in Leipzig by Commander Rosen, Inspector for Repatriation Missions, to serve as a liaison officer between the HQ of the American XXI Corps and the French repatriation services on the one hand, and the Soviet authorities on the other.

My mission with the American army ended in August, so I went back to Paris on August 10, 1945, and after one week spent getting my military situation sorted out, I left again for Berlin, where I have been ever since.

That was the first time I had been back to France since June 4, 1940, the day I was captured by the Germans.

I am enclosing an affidavit given to me by the XXI Corps, which served as the basis for a nomination for the Bronze Star Medal.

I consider the above declaration to be of a nature to clear me of the first two counts against me.

As for the third one, regarding membership in the organization commonly known as "La Cagoule," I solemnly swear as follows:

At the beginning of the year 1936, I took part in a "study group" organized by a newly founded political party whose propaganda posters had been posted on the walls in my neighborhood. The party was called, if I remember correctly, the National Revolutionary Party.

The construction company where I was working sent me out into the provinces during the months of March and April, and I went back to the rue Caumartin during the month of May. I found the police on the premises, and they let me go after a brief interrogation.

One month later I was called to the criminal investigation department where, after another interrogation, I was released.

I was again traveling away from Paris for my work, and I totally forgot about this affair.

Four months later, in October, 1936, I was called up for my military service. I reenlisted in 1938, and served in the Army uninterruptedly from October 15, 1936 until August 15, 1945, the date I went back to Paris and was demobbed.

I certify that the only time between 1936 and this day that I ever heard again of that unfortunate incident was in 1938, when as a sub-lieutenant with the eighth cavalry in Saint-Germain-en-Laye, I received the visit of two inspectors from the Sûreté who questioned me on my affiliation with "La Cagoule." I consider that my explanations were sufficient at the time to prove there was no foundation to their allegations, since I never heard anything further about the matter.

I would like to take this opportunity to reassert and insist that neither before nor during my military service did I belong to La Cagoule, and I have never committed any act that might be harmful to the interests of my country or contrary to my honor as an officer.

It is on my honor as an officer, which I have never betrayed, that I make this declaration.

The years I have spent serving my country and the blood I have shed for her give me the right to request that I be allowed to clear my name publicly of these accusations.

Berlin, February 26, 1946.

Jean Wiazemsky.

March 4, 1946

Dear Mama,

This will be a quick little note because I'll be leaving any minute for Leipzig and I just found out that someone is going to Paris. I tried to call you several times but couldn't get through.

We don't know anything definite yet, but we have received reassurance from several sides at once. The French police in Berlin have taken the matter in hand and assure us that everything will work out.

Wia is a little bit more relaxed. Not much, but, well, a little bit. There's no point in me telling you that lately I haven't been swimming in happiness the way the people I saw in Paris predicted. Poor Yvan is even more desperate for my sake than for his own. As long as this matter is not settled, and settled properly, he won't hear of us getting married. I've been doing everything I can to restore his confidence both in life and in himself, but it's hard. He had such a blissful expression on his face the day I arrived and now he's completely withdrawn, and it's not a happy sight.

What do you think of all this? What has Papa done?

There is a lot of work. It's very cold.

Ask Papa to forgive me, to forgive us, but I assure you that poor Wia has nothing to do with this and he really is miserable. And he's not the sort of person who can just brush it off lightly.

Sending you all my love,

Your little Claire.

It is not even six o'clock in the morning. As soon as she has sealed her envelope, Claire goes down to the girls' floor to put it by the door to the room of a still sleeping colleague who will be leaving for Paris later in the day. She has already put on her coat and boots because Mistou is waiting for her at the wheel of their ambulance, together with Wia. They are part of a convoy of four vehicles headed for Leipzig: in a makeshift hospital being used by the Soviets, there has been a sudden, virulent outbreak of typhus. According to sources that, for the moment, must remain secret, there are French prisoners among the infected. A first British medical team is already on site and has reported numerous deaths; those who have already had typhus or who are in recovery and no longer contagious must be evacuated, immediately.

With Claire there, they can leave. At her request, Mistou lets her drive. On his lap Wia has a rough map of the area around Berlin, and he is fulminating about which route to take. He maintains that if they had gone another way the roads would have been smoother. If he's not fussing against whoever it was that chose this route, it's the endless rain. Instinctively, Claire and Mistou both know better than to say anything and risk making him even crosser. They can tell he's tense, on edge; he's lost all sense of humor. This is the first time they've ever seen him like this. Will he at least be able to convince the Soviets to hand over the French prisoners? They know it can take hours, and that Wia will have to deploy all his charm and diplomacy. For the time being his main concern seems to be to compile a list of names of those who can attest to his innocence. He has already managed to find a few, with Rosen. They are waiting impatiently for the affidavits from the American generals.

It is still dark, the convoy is making slow progress. Finally the day breaks. Wrecks of charred tanks still litter the sides of a nonexistent road. Famished crows fly overhead and their lugubrious cries accentuate the desolation of the fields and plains.

Hours later they reach the outskirts of Leipzig and what remains of its buildings. Some are totally destroyed, others are still more or less standing, but not a single one has a roof. The remaining walls, without exception, have been blackened by smoke from the fires. There is no one in the street to see the convoy go by. As in Berlin, the German survivors seem to be disappearing underground in the presence of the victors. Claire, Mistou, and Wia have already been on missions to this region, and they are dismayed to see how little has changed. The silence that greets them is still the silence of a dead city.

They pull over when they are near the Soviets' makeshift hospital: it consists of old buildings adjacent to a prison camp, now surrounded by a quarantine line and guarded by a large number of armed sentries.

"Let's go," says Wia. "We'll find out soon enough."

By late afternoon, after hours of deliberation with the Soviet authorities, their chances of finding any Frenchmen seem hopeless. Claire, Mistou, and their comrades have been taking shelter in their ambulances to keep out of the pouring rain while they wait. They are cold and hungry, and watch worriedly as mud and water inundate the roads.

Suddenly Wia appears, radiant, in the company of the Soviet officer.

"It's all settled, get out the stretchers, girls."

Soon afterward the ambulance sets off on its return journey, with Mistou at the wheel. Night has fallen and the cars' headlights struggle to show the way along the flooded roads. Squeezed together in the front seat with Mistou, Claire and Wia peer into the darkness, looking out for ditches and potholes. In the back, former workers from the STO occupy three of the four bunk beds. They have already had typhus; they're still weak but no longer contagious. "They're alive!" says Claire regularly. "Alive!" echoes Mistou. For a brief spell they have forgotten their hunger, cold, and fatigue.

During the rare moments when the driving is easier, Wia explains how he was able to rescue the men.

"There was one officer who made it all possible through his intervention, Alexei Gazdanov—we'd been prisoners together, with thirty or so other Soviet soldiers. We all got along very well. Red, White, proletarian or aristocrat, what difference does it make, we could all speak the same language! They really took me under their wing, going around calling me 'Comrade Prince,' no less! When we were liberated by the Red Army, I fought alongside them, and then they explained my case to the authorities. They eventually took me back to the Americans, but not before suggesting I go return to the Soviet Union with them . . . oh, Claire?"

Claire had fallen asleep, and didn't hear Wia's story. Shooting in the dark, she ventures a reply: "Yes, and then?"

"And I was tempted, really tempted. While I was together with them in the camp I understood how pointless it was to want to go back and rebuild Russia the way it used to be. I put in a request to go to the USSR with my parents, but the Soviets refused. While I may have been redeemed in their eyes by my conduct, my parents, in their opinion, were still traitors. That's why I stayed in the West."

He can feel Claire's head growing heavy on his shoulder, her brown curls grazing his cheek: he realizes she has gone back to sleep.

The next morning, Claire, Mistou, Plumette, and two Belgian ambulance drivers meet for a late breakfast in the kitchen on the first floor. They are discussing the day's agenda, and what to do about the three French workers who've been admitted temporarily in the Berlin hospital. The door to the apartment opens slowly and a young girl with very strong Slavic features appears in the doorway.

Her name is Olga, she is of Russian origin and became French before the war. Like Wia, she speaks several languages fluently. Léon de Rosen took her on as extra staff to work as a translator whenever they have one of their numerous meetings with Allied representatives. Her reliability and devotion to the cause of displaced persons have made her indispensable. She arrived in mid-January, and before long she had befriended the girls from the French and Belgian Red Cross; they often invite her to join them at mealtimes. Claire knows Olga works in the same office as Wia but she hasn't yet had time to get to know her.

"This is for you," says Olga. "A note from Wia."

She hands her a piece of paper folded in four, takes the cup of tea Plumette pours for her and sits down at their table. While Claire is reading, the kitchen is silent. So silent that you can hear the sounds from the street, the rare sound of cars going by. Once she finishes reading, Claire gives a long dramatic sigh and shrugs her shoulders. Then she says, plaintively, "Unbelievable."

"What is it, sweetheart?"

As her answer is slow in coming, Mistou turns to her other companions, "It is unbelievable how often she says, 'unbelievable!'"

Their laughter is the nudge that Claire needs.

"Wia writes here that the testimony of an American general has completely cleared him of the accusations of illicit trafficking with the Germans. The general certifies that Wia was a prisoner during the entire war, and fought alongside the Soviets, etc., etc., etc. Any normal person ought to be really happy, but Wia, no. He is obsessed by the allegations that he belonged to La Cagoule, and he goes on and on about his tarnished honor, etc., etc., etc."

"You cannot understand."

It's Olga the newcomer who has just spoken in such a hesitant yet firm voice. The slight blush on her cheeks and an imperceptible trembling through her entire body betray what it has cost her to speak. The silence that greets her words seems to oppress her even more, and she seems to hesitate to say anything more. But after Plumette makes an encouraging gesture she takes a deep breath and says, "You have always been French. You cannot imagine what it's like to have to leave everything behind—your house, your belongings, your homeland, everything. You cannot imagine what it's like to wander from one country to the next, having to change your language, your culture. How could you possibly understand what it means to be stateless? You have to have been in his shoes to understand. Stateless . . . I am sure the word doesn't mean a thing to you . . . So when at last you find a country that is willing to take you in, a country that is offering you a chance to start all over again from scratch, well, you cling to it, you want to show you are worthy. And when that same country honors you by granting you French nationality, it's your duty to be perfect, and to serve your country a hundred, a thousand times better than any French-born citizen could. Wia cannot bear to think that with this Cagoule business they might suspect him of having turned against the established order of his adopted country. You must all make an effort, try to understand how proud he is to be French, try to understand why his pride has been wounded and why he will not rest until his name has been cleared. Officially."

Olga spoke all in one go, without taking a breath, her face getting redder and redder. Now drops of sweat are pearling on her forehead. The other young women stare at her in silence, transfixed. Then she smiles, a little embarrassed smile in guise of an apology as she turns to Claire.

"Please don't be cross with me for speaking so passionately, Claire. I'm very shy and like all shy people, when I get going . . . And anyway I was speaking to the others as much as to you. It's for Wia's sake, so that you'll understand him better . . . You above all, Claire, he loves you so much! Claire?"

But Claire seems to be elsewhere, lost in a strange reverie. She does this sometimes, she goes far, far away.

The moon is high in the sky, lighting their way as if it were broad daylight. After the German pine forests come the French pine forests and fields. Claire is driving, she's not tired, but buoyed, rather, by a certain cheerfulness she often feels when she is driving through the night. Through the open window she breathes in the fresh air and an occasional whiff of trees and earth: it helps her to stay awake. She is whistling popular tunes, and the various national anthems she has learned in Berlin. It is as if she were leaving winter behind and were on her way to greet the springtime, to greet a free, harmonious, peaceful life. She almost forgets that she is not alone in the car.

In the back, Wia and Léon de Rosen are sound asleep. One of them makes a whistling sound as he breathes, the other is snoring from time to time. They have taken turns with the driving since they left Berlin late that afternoon. The last three hundred kilometers to Paris are Claire's. She decided they should share like this, and the two men went along with her. Now in the deceptive silence of the night, Claire can think more calmly about the reason behind this trip.

It is turning out to be harder than anyone could ever have imagined to prove that Wia never belonged to the extreme right wing movement La Cagoule. In Paris, at the Ministry of Justice, unidentified individuals are still obstructing the case. Léon de Rosen has come out in defense of his friend as if it were his own case. He is a brave man, used to being obeyed and to being unanimously appreciated. He holds justice to be a concrete requirement, part of one's everyday struggle in life.

But Léon de Rosen is not always diplomatic: sometimes he gets carried away by his subjectivity, regardless of the person he is dealing with, including Wia. Claire thinks back over the ideas they exchanged during the early part of the trip. She has already forgotten the details, but she remembers that Léon recommended having Wia confront his accusers.

Wia thought it was too early, the situation was still too unclear. But when Claire was ordered to take an ambulance back to Paris urgently, he put his argument aside, and the two of them decided to go along with her. Wia, more superstitious than ever, saw this chance occurrence as a positive nod from fate, the first sign that his lucky star was on its way back to him. "I'll let them out wherever they want, drop the car off at the garage, and then I'll go to see my parents," thinks Claire breezily. She already has a seat in a return flight that afternoon, and she's looking forward to being back in Berlin that very evening.

The sun rises above the peaceful, dew-covered countryside. Claire drives through still-sleeping villages; only the roosters have begun to crow. She thinks she can detect the perfume of flowers, and the smell of bread baking. She is surprised to discover landscapes where the traces of war are already fading, or others that have been miraculously spared. She feels a deep love for the countryside of her native land. In a hushed voice, so that she will not wake up the two sleeping men, she sings Charles Trenet:

Le vent dans les bois fait hou hou hou
La biche aux abois fait mê mê mê
La vaisselle cassée fait cric crin crac
Et les pieds mouillés font flic flic flac
Mais . . .

Boum
Quand votre coeur fait boum.[6]

"No, Wia, I can't, no . . . "

Claire has dropped Rosen off in Paris and is about to leave Wia, too, when he suddenly asks her to go with him to see his parents. Claire objects that they haven't been forewarned, they won't be expecting her—to meet for the first time they must be better prepared, notified well ahead of time. Wia talks about Russian hospitality. He sweeps away all her arguments one by one. He insists, with a feverish passion that is new to her, as if it were a matter of life or death, as if it were the greatest proof of love she could give him. She protests that she hasn't slept, that she needs to wash and fix her hair and put on some makeup; she needs to change out of her travel-creased clothing into something more elegant.

"I have to do you credit, Wia . . . First impressions are so important . . . it's, it's . . . decisive!"

"You're never lovelier than in your Red Cross uniform."

Claire is too weary to protest further, so she allows herself to be led to the building on the rue Raynouard where Wia's family lives. While they wait for the elevator, he embraces her passionately, covering her face with kisses.

"I'm so happy that you're going to meet my parents at last. So happy . . . "

Wia rings the bell a first time, then again, then the third time more insistently. He is suddenly very nervous and impatient.

---

[6] *The wind in the trees goes hoo hoo hoo*
The cow in the field says moo moo moo
Broken dishes go bing bang crash
And my wet feet go splish splosh splash
But...

Boom
Hear how your heart goes boom.

"What the hell are they doing . . . "

From the other side of the door they can hear confused sounds, some shuffling to and fro, murmuring. Finally the door opens and Wia steps into the apartment. Claire has stayed out on the landing, frozen; standing before her are two elderly people in their dressing gowns, and behind them she can see an untidy room, with the remnants of a meal still on the table. Who is this woman in curlers, her features weary, staring at Claire with the same shocked, surprised expression on her face?

Claire is half sitting, half lying on a bench on the rue Fontaine, prey to an animal panic. Passersby suppose she has had a sudden malaise and stop to offer help, but when they encounter her fierce silence and hostile gaze, they continue on their way, resigned. "A broken heart," murmurs one of them.

The words echo in her ears. She repeats them several times, the better to grasp their meaning. Because she is forcing herself to breathe slowly, gradually the vice around her chest relaxes and memories rush in as sharp as photographs. She sees Wia's parents, their apartment. Two words run through her head like a refrain: ugliness and poverty, poverty and ugliness. It did not take her even ten minutes to register how messy the room was, how ill assorted the furnishings; everywhere were shawls, etchings, knickknacks that seemed horribly tacky to her. But if only that were everything . . . Above all, she sees his parents. In her own flesh she can sense how humiliated they must have felt to be caught unawares like that, in their threadbare dressing gowns full of cigarette holes. How could Wia have imagined even for one instant that they might enjoy a surprise visit like that? Could he not see the tears in his mother's eyes, the awkward gestures she was making to try to remove her ridiculous curlers . . . It was Claire who, in a surge of pity, sincere pity, instinctively went up to the woman to embrace her and apologize for their unfortunate intrusion. And didn't she agree to have tea, and the tea service was fine porcelain, but so very old and chipped . . . Then she took her leave, on the pretext that she had to drop off her vehicle at the garage. How relieved they seemed . . . Almost eager, as they followed her out onto the landing . . . And Wia, looking blissfully happy . . .

"What an idiot!" says Claire out loud. "What a complete and utter idiot!" she thinks angrily, bitterly; at no point did he seem to feel even the least bit ill at ease, nor did he realize that both she and his parents were terror-stricken. He was the one who'd concocted their sudden meeting, and he had simply assumed it would be a happy one—and no doubt to his eyes it had been. His very blindness was enough to turn the whole disastrous morning into a tragedy. A ridiculous tragedy.

Claire lights a cigarette. With icy lucidity she compares her family to Wia's. It's not just their two different nationalities—they live in two completely different worlds. On her bench on the rue La Fontaine, she is exactly halfway between the apartment at 38 Avenue Théophile Gautier and the apartment at 12bis, rue Raynouard. This ironic geographical coincidence fails to make her laugh: it merely reminds her of her agenda for the morning. Hadn't she also planned a surprise visit to her own parents', to share her unexpected presence in Paris with them, however briefly? For a moment she steps outside herself to imagine what it would be like to announce to them that she has broken her engagement. Because that is exactly what she is contemplating. Other images assail her and she sees herself as she was a year ago, on another bench near the Pont Alexandre III, engaged to Patrice and discovering that she didn't want to marry him. And today the same stifling sensation of being trapped has come over her. "It's history repeating itself," she says several times. She feels an overwhelming desire to weep. And she hears again what the passersby said just a few minutes ago: "A broken heart."

Back in Berlin, in the floozies' room, Claire is tossing and turning. Mistou is taking up nearly all the bed, her sleep is restless, and she mutters an endless string of words, moaning, prey to bad dreams. The dog Kitz is stretched out his full length on the carpet and from time to time he grunts. He was overjoyed to see Claire when she arrived, and she responded gratefully. She said nothing to any of the girls about her meeting with Wia's parents, and she lied about her own parents. How could she confess that she didn't even go to see them, that she had ended up walking by herself along the Seine, smoking one cigarette after the other? During that long aimless stroll she took the full measure of everything that divided her from Wia, everything that might make their marriage impossible. She also decided not to discuss it with anyone, or do anything until Wia's name had been completely cleared. After that, she would see.

Wia came back the next afternoon. Rosen had stayed behind in Paris, to obtain the last necessary documents. The two men are confident: before long the file will be closed and they'll be able to set the date of the wedding. Wia is so happy that he urges Claire to come with him on a walk in the forest.

After the long winter, spring seems to have come early. The ruins of Berlin look quite different in the sunlight. People fill the streets and the forests near the city.

Wia is holding Claire by the waist, and they walk briskly through the first trees. To Claire it is intoxicating—the heady smell of resin and earth, the dappled light in the branches, the unexpected softness of the air. Tender green shoots bring their promise of flowers. Claire makes plans for her days off. A few weeks from now, perhaps two, they will come back here and pick snowdrops, violets, and primroses. She even agrees to learn to ride horseback because it is Wia's favorite sport. The farther they go into the forest, the less her future seems to threaten. She has not forgotten the encounter with Wia's parents, but now that she has left Paris behind and is in his arms, the rest does not seem so important. His parents are two poor ghosts, while Wia is a man of flesh and blood, alive, so alive.

Kitz is with them, running far ahead.

"Oh how distracted I am! I nearly forgot to give you what I went to get in Paris," says Wia.

He removes a worn little box from his coat pocket and hands it to Claire. As she hesitates to open it, he does it for her, taking a ring from the box and sliding it onto the ring finger of her left hand.

"It was my mother's engagement ring. She never wanted to sell it because it was meant for my future wife. It's yours now."

Impressed, Claire looks at the golden ring set with little rubies and diamonds.

Wia writes to Madame François Mauriac.

Berlin, March 28

Madame,

I just found out that one of our officers will be leaving for Paris in a short while, and I wanted to use the opportunity to dash off a note to you that I would not have entrusted to the normal mail service.

This morning Claire got a letter from you that upset her a great deal, and I myself am fairly worried, as Claire did share a few passages with me. To be honest, there's one sentence in particular that has filled us with dismay, the sentence where you say, more or less, "Things have not gone very well here." Claire and I have been wondering with a certain anxiety whether this—along with Rosen's "lack of tact"—is in reference to his conversation with Monsieur Mauriac or his meeting with the minister.

Rosen is a first-class fellow and I hope you will have a better opportunity to judge and appreciate his true worth. Having said that, he can be very abrupt, but he makes up for his errors of tact and diplomacy, or at least tries to, through his Slavic charm and his indisputable allure.

That is why I must apologize for telling you quite frankly that Claire and I, as paradoxical as it might seem, would prefer to know that it was with you that Rosen behaved clumsily.

Just before he left, Claire and I had a long conversation with him, and he remains optimistic regarding the outcome of my "affair." In Paris he's supposed to see a lot of very important people in order to deal with it once and for all. Is that what he has done? What were the results? I have no idea, because I haven't called him for over a week. I'll call him tonight, and only then will I know the nature of this dilemma caused by your letter this morning.

The "war of nerves" has been revived, but this time I'm the one who's calm and Claire is upset, and that is why she won't write to you until after tonight's telephone call.

She and I both feel guilty toward you. Claire is an unnatural daughter, and until the day I become your son—even an unnatural one—I am simply an uncouth individual for not having written to you. But both of us have been working very hard, and as idiotic as it may seem, I have already passed on one of my faults to Claire, which is that of being superstitious. After our letters, which may have been a tad panicky the first day, we didn't dare reassure you too quickly when things were beginning to look like they might work out, for fear of bringing a new misfortune down upon us.

I can confirm to you that there is one thing that hasn't changed since I wrote to Monsieur Mauriac, at the beginning of the affair. Despite Claire's insistence, I refuse to get married until I am sure of the outcome. But I think we will know before the 10-15 of April. If things go badly, I will go back to Paris with Claire and while she has a rest, I'll see what might still be done. I have the feeling I will be bad tempered and in the mood for a fight. But if the outcome is good, then and only then can our plan to get married in May go ahead.

At the beginning of April there is going to be a rehabilitation of the French in the division in Berlin. If I am rehabilitated life will be wonderful, everything will be fine again and I believe that will be enough of a guarantee. If I am not rehabilitated, that will mean that the black hand has prevailed for the time being, and I will go back to Paris in fine form and spoiling for a fight.

Forgive me for breaking off here, but the person who's leaving is as restless as a circus horse and I've sworn I won't make him miss his train.

Just one more word about our life here. Claire had a bad spell of indigestion but she's recovering, and she complains bitterly that I persecute her because I tried to stop her from smoking and staying up late. The weather is marvelous and I make her get up at six in the morning to go riding at half past seven, and this will oblige her sooner or later to go to bed early. In the afternoon when it's just the two of us, and almost every Sunday, we go for long walks through the woods.

I have a great deal of work and Claire thinks she can behave tyrannically, acting like a very desperate widow on the pretext that I don't look after her enough.

Again, please forgive me for my silence. I kiss your hands, and convey my deepest respect and affection.

Yvan.

Wia has been writing his letter in one go, with Claire standing behind him trying to read it. From time to time she comments on a sentence here or there, but Wia doesn't listen, he is in too great a hurry. The young officer with his suitcase in his hand is already on the landing.

"Hang on a sec, I'm finished!" Wia shouts.

But just as he has finished the letter at last, and is slipping it into the envelope, Claire grabs it and in a furious tiny handwriting adds next to the date, "I'm not so much upset as angry. Thank heavens, I'll only write to you tomorrow. Sending all my love, all the same. Claire." Then she runs to catch up with the messenger in the stairway, before she goes back up to Wia's office.

"You're much too kind with her, using kid gloves, you're only encouraging her to act stupid, as if she didn't understand, and . . . "

Claire is so annoyed that she cannot find her words. She collapses in a chair, lights a cigarette, and stares at Wia with her dark, furious eyes. He is surprised by her violent reaction and doesn't know what to say. To disguise his lack of composure he opens one of the many files cluttering his desk.

"I'm polite with your mother, that's all," he says neutrally.

"She doesn't deserve it!"

Her exclamation sounds so much like adolescent rebelliousness that Wia feels an irrepressible desire to laugh welling up inside. Still looking down at his file, he doesn't give anything away, while Claire continues to rant, sulkily.

"Not only did Mama write three pages reproaching me for

not giving her any news, not only does she continue to ignore my work and seems to think I am spending too long a *vacation* in Berlin, but on top of it in the midst of all this mess she comes out with her ambiguous sentence. When she says, 'I had a visit from Léon de Rosen,' and won't go beyond 'Here things have not gone very well'—what on earth is she talking about? About Rosen's visit to the Ministry just before he saw her? About her conversation with Rosen? Or perhaps she just doesn't like him? As for the PS, it takes the cake! To end such a letter with nothing more than 'If the wedding goes ahead your father and I would prefer to have the ceremony in Paris,' when she knows perfectly well that our honeymoon will be in Germany, and she knows how much we both want the wedding to be in Berlin, it's . . . it's . . . "

"Unbelievable!"

"You took the words from my mouth."

Wia cannot help but laugh, amused by Claire's tirade. Claire is annoyed at first, then relents and goes to sit on his lap.

"Still," she says proudly, "I didn't sign the letter with the usual 'Your little Claire.' Just Claire, nothing else. I think that must be the first time . . . "

It is already late in the evening when Claire and Wia take Kitz out for a walk. Although it is dark, a few passersby still linger in the street. Allied soldiers for the most part, but also local people. It is as if the approach of spring had roused the ruined city from a long sleep.

Claire and Wia walk slowly, holding each other close. They are weary of all the tension accumulated during the day, but they feel happy and calm at last. Rosen just called them: the La Cagoule case has been closed, and Wia's name has been cleared. They are planning a party to celebrate their victory and the talent of their negotiator.

"But still," says Claire, "he almost caused us to have a falling out with Mama . . . and if he takes it on himself to plead for our wedding to be held in Berlin, I fear the worst!"

"You always see everything in black, my darling. But I warn you: I want an optimistic wife who doesn't have migraines."

Saturday, April 27, 1946
My dear little Mama,
News from you at last. I was really beginning to think you had completely forgotten your little girl.

If I haven't written it's because until this morning I've hardly had a minute.

A fine and a fairly pious Holy Week: no cigarettes or any other good things on Holy Wednesday or Good Friday. I was going round in circles, completely crazy. On Maundy Thursday we all went to confession. On Friday we had a very fine sermon and on Easter Sunday a magnificent mass at eleven o'clock where almost everyone from number 96 took communion.

In the night from Saturday to Sunday we went to the Orthodox midnight mass. It was very moving because we were all crowded together in the little Russian church, with Orthodox Germans, American, British, French and even Russian Red Army uniforms. All the same faces and same voices, just wearing different uniforms. Next to me was a young German woman, and she was crying as she chanted "Christ is risen"; I was on the verge of tears myself.

On Tuesday morning I left on a mission at nine o'clock and came back again at two o'clock in the morning. I drove the entire time and I was tired but content, because my ambulance was full of people who were happy to be going home.

Dinner with the Russians, naturally, and a great personal victory because it was actually the Russians who stopped me from drinking for once. Normally they try to make you drink one vodka after another.

But this time, I managed to swap my full glass for an empty one, and then I pretended to drink it straight down and made all the faces such an exploit requires. Then, before their admiring gazes I asked for another one. But the man who was with me in my ambulance categorically refused because he was so afraid I'd end up putting him in the ditch.

On Thursday we set off for Frankfurt-an-der-Oder with six ambulances and a truck to go and fetch 208 Alsatians, Belgians, and Dutch whom the Russians, after a million requests, finally agreed to hand over to us. You can imagine the expressions on the faces of all those detainees when we arrived. All these lads who had not been able to send any news to their parents for two years or more—and they insisted that there are still many Alsatians detained by the Russians. It was a triumphant return for everybody, except me, because I was getting an upset stomach. No need to tell you about the night that followed and the next day.

Today I'm fine again and I'm writing in a great rush because someone will be taking the plane before long.

Things are fine with Wia and me. We're both a little sad we can't get married on May 5. Wia went to Paris for one day regarding his affair. They acknowledged that there had been a case of mistaken identity, that he wasn't the one who'd been trafficking with the Germans and the only reason they dragged up the La Cagoule business was because of that. Moreover, Wia's new citation produced the desired effect, and he left again confident that everything had been settled. But we'll only really know for sure once his contract has been renewed, which should be very soon.

I am glad you had a good stay in Malagar. Papa must be all suntanned and younger than ever.

I'll write soon, Mama, I send all my hugs and kisses and will be in touch. Forgive me for this letter, but I have so little time. The weather is beautiful. Sending all my love to everyone.

Claire, Mistou, and Rolanne have been designated for a nighttime mission, so they have the day for themselves and have decided to go for a stroll through Berlin without any male escorts. Everyday life is improving, and security instructions have relaxed somewhat, but they must stay together and keep an eye out for each other. This is the second time they've been out without coats, and with the warm late April air they feel like they're on vacation. They are young, beautiful, and respected by all: in the space of a few months, the soldiers of the different Allied forces have come to appreciate both their charm and their hard work. The French Red Cross is enjoying unprecedented prestige, the girls know it and walk proudly, pleased to be looking so good in their uniforms.

Mistou is the most radiant of all. She beams her brilliant smile on anyone—to charm them, or be pleasant, she herself doesn't really know for sure. But she enjoys the American soldiers' admiring whistles, and thanks them with a wink that is not altogether innocent. Her friends just laugh, not the least bit jealous.

The ruins of Berlin look completely different in the bright sunshine. In broad daylight you can see the city's wounds, the poverty and hardship the inhabitants continue to endure. It is a cruel slight, but there is something strangely grand about it, too. Between two destroyed buildings, at the back of a forgotten courtyard, daffodils and lilac bushes are in bloom. Their perfume hangs heavy in the air and for a brief moment the terrible smell of gutters and death seems to vanish. Awestruck, the three girls cease their chatter. At an intersection they run into Hilde, the interpreter from the early days, who still works with them. Though she sometimes speaks with Rolanne, she is as reserved as ever, and won't tell them anything about her life. Now she nods her head briefly in greeting, then quickens her step and disappears down a side street. "What a pity," says Rolanne. "I would have so liked to invite her to join us."

Back at the apartment, Claire finds a letter addressed to her on the kitchen table where she is sure to see it. She immediately recognizes Rosen's handwriting and opens the envelope apprehensively. Then she reads, and reads again the typewritten sheet as if she could not make up her mind.

"It's Rosen, he's written to my parents about the wedding," she says at last. "It's entitled 'Different aspects of the wedding problem.' It's a nice letter, wordy and maniacal, and maybe it will be of use, I can't tell."

Mistou sets a cup of tea down before her, sits down next to Claire and says with friendly authority, "Read us the letter, we'll tell you."

Claire hesitates, then decides to go ahead.

"Okay then, just bits of it, because it's very long. I'll skip over the beginning where he reminds us that 'As of April 1 there has been a rotation of fixed senior staff in Berlin.' What that basically means is that in the best case, Wia will become a civil servant, with guaranteed employment, a brighter future, and he'll be a more acceptable son-in-law, etc. Then he explains that the wedding must take place as soon as possible—he underlines this. I quote: 'Sentimental reasons: this really only concerns Wia and Claire, but they would be grateful if this was taken into consideration. Theoretical reasons (I remind you, this is unimportant): their engagement has already been fairly long, and a lot of people know about it—no point having people talk. Practical reason of paramount importance: June is the month of the French presidential elections and it would be difficult, if not impossible, for Wia to get leave in June. So the wedding must take place either before May 15 or at the end of June.' But the most interesting thing is what he says about where the wedding is to be held. I quote, 'Berlin, pros: 1. Congenial atmosphere, they have nothing but friends in Berlin, none of whom could come to Paris and would be very disappointed (many of them Allies). 2. Would make things extremely easy to prepare, etc.. The entire division will take part. 3. Considerable savings. 4. French propaganda vis-à-vis Allies. Visit by Monsieur François Mauriac to Berlin. Possibility he might give a lecture. Paris, pros: Possibility of inviting all and sundry relatives. Advantage debatable from Claire and Wia's point of view, but probably a very real one from parents' point of view. Paris, cons: 1. Genuine disappointment for Claire and Wia. 2. Absence of almost all their friends, French and Allied. 3. More or less absolute requirement to hold a "grand wedding," which would be: boring, costly, complicated, source of hurt feelings (people left off the list), unavoidably public, something Monsieur François Mauriac seems to fear in the wake of the scandal. 4. Lack of cars. 5. Host of complicated preparations. 6. Choice of church will be tricky. The ideal would be either a wedding in both churches, or a Catholic wedding with Orthodox rite. Both of which would be difficult to arrange in Paris. 7. Sartorial complications (above all for Wia). Having said this, naturally it is out of the question to ignore any veto on the part of the parents regarding Berlin, the point being simply to explain to them how much Claire and Wia would prefer a wedding in Berlin.' So, girls, what do you think?"

Rolanne is nodding her head, with a faint dreamy smile. As always, she is taking the question seriously and giving herself time to think. Mistou, more quickly, adopts a solemn expression and in a strange masculine voice, with an effort to sound hoarse she says, "Your plea, Monsieur de Rosen, has convinced us, my wife and I. Our daughter shall marry Yvan in Berlin as she wishes. Moreover, I am greatly looking forward to meeting the charm squadron of the French Red Cross, those sexy . . . "

That's as far as she can get with her imitation of François Mauriac, and she collapses with laughter, joined by Claire and Rolanne.

"Am I interrupting?"

The three friends did not see Olga arrive: now she is standing discreetly in the doorway. She just got back the night before from a trip to Paris to celebrate Easter with her family. In her hand is a tiny pink package wrapped in a purple ribbon that she now holds out to Claire.

"This is for you," she says. "From Princess Wiazemsky."

As if they have suddenly remembered they need to be somewhere else, Rolanne and Mistou get up and leave the kitchen. Olga pulls over a chair and sits down next to Claire, her eyes shining with anticipation.

Claire has opened the package and now in her palm she is rolling a tiny golden egg.

"It is our custom to give an egg-shaped jewel to celebrate Easter. Yours is quite modest, because it doesn't have any gems, just a hand-painted Cyrillic cross, but it is a Fabergé all the same. Women add one charm every year to the same chain. I don't know how many your future mother-in-law has, but I'll bet she took that one from her collection to give it to you. It's a quiet way of introducing you to our customs. I know you wear a medal with the Virgin around your neck—would you like to add this little egg to the chain? Here, let me help you . . . Wia will be so happy."

Olga removes the chain, adds the little golden egg, and fastens it again around Claire's neck. Claire submits without saying a word or making a gesture, without showing the slightest emotion. Olga is surprised, then concerned by her lack of reaction.

"Is something wrong?"

"I think you ought to marry Wia, not me."

"Oh, Claire! How can you say anything so stupid?"

"It's the truth. You share the same language, the same culture, the same history. Wia and I are from two different planets . . . "

Claire stares at Olga provocatively. She watches as her cheeks flush red and her expression is overwhelmed by distress. What Claire has just said is something she sincerely believes, even if she knows she may only be expressing a fleeting, unimportant thought. She is perfectly aware, moreover, that she is being unfair, because she thinks she has guessed Olga's secret: the girl is falling in love with Léon de Rosen. And she doesn't even realize, Claire thinks, suddenly weary. But Olga has recovered her composure: standing before Claire, she breaks the silence with feverish conviction.

"I saw Sophie Wiazemsky at Easter Mass on the rue Daru. We stopped to talk, and she told me about the surprise visit and the, shall we say, circumstances under which you met."

Upon hearing her words, Claire does not try to hide her surprise. She starts to speak, but Olga interrupts her.

"Wia is an intelligent man, but in that instance he behaved like an idiot, an absurd idiot—his love for you has blinded him to a certain reality. If they had been warned ahead of time, you would have been given a magnificent reception. As it is . . . "

Olga can't find her words. She knows Claire is looking at her closely, begging her to continue.

" . . . as it is, the fact remains that his parents are trying to get over four years of war and deprivation, and they are poor, and they will always be people who have lost their roots. You see, that is what you must always bear in mind."

Claire is on her feet. The two women look at each other, very aware of the importance of Olga's words, and of the quality of their friendship.

"Thank you," murmurs Claire, reaching to embrace her.

On Friday, July 5, 1946, at half past eleven in the morning, Claire climbs the steps of the Church of Notre Dame d'Auteuil on her father's arm. Her tense smile is trying to hide a painful migraine. She cannot hear the flattering commentary of the neighborhood residents, she has no idea how pretty she is, with her dark hair against her white dress. And she is angry. An anger she shares with her father, with Wia, their two families and their friends.

Because Wia is Orthodox, the Catholic Church has refused to celebrate the wedding. Despite François Mauriac's intervention, despite his notoriety, all the young couple are entitled to is a blessing. Not in the nave of the church but in the sacristy, as if on the sly. François Mauriac is displeased, and everyone can see on his closed face how much he disapproves of what he considers too strict an attitude on the part of his church.

The ceremony does not take long. Claire often turns to her mother as if to reassure herself over and over of her support. She is very grateful to her for helping her prepare this day she has been dreading. She has forgiven her for refusing to allow the wedding to be held in Berlin, where everything would have been simpler. Her love for her mother is boundless, and on this day, in the sacristy, she loves her like a little girl. It would not take much to make her weep at the thought of leaving her. Already earlier this morning she burst into tears, great heaving sobs, before she put on her white gown. But her mother was ready with tender words, words her daughter needed in order—according to her favorite expression—to *fare bella figura*. "But how can I *fare bella figura* with a migraine?" thinks Claire, desperate. She can hear Wia fussing in her ear, "They're making us get married in a broom closet!"

Fortunately once they leave the church, the atmosphere changes dramatically.

The girls from 96 Kurfürstendamm, dressed in their uniforms, have formed a guard of honor for the young couple: at last the ceremony is filled with happiness, thanks to their joy and emotion. Other friends who were able to come from Berlin have gathered at the bottom of the steps and are applauding wildly. There are the French officers from the Displaced Persons Section, clustered around their leader, Léon de Rosen, who cannot help but show how proud he is. "I'm the one who made it all happen!" he says over and over again, to whomever will listen. Claire and Wia, in a shower of rice, pose for the numerous photographers. Contrary to everything they wanted for their wedding, "François Mauriac's Daughter Weds Authentic Russian Prince" is something of a high-society event.

A second ceremony is held later at the Russian Orthodox Cathedral of Saint Alexander Nevsky on the rue Daru. For the first time, Claire's family becomes acquainted with the Orthodox liturgy, its chants and prayers. Furtively, they gaze at the high round dome, the iconostasis, the painted frescoes and numerous icons. A multitude of candles cast a gentle glow on people's faces, making last traces of the war vanish, making even the wrinkles of the elderly vanish. Claire can tell that her migraine is leaving her at last, and a feeling of joy begins to spread through her veins. The beauty and fervor of this religious ceremony have effaced all the pettiness of the earlier one. An occasional glance at her parents is enough to reassure her: they, too, at last, seem happy to see their daughter married in this church, and according to this rite.

Later, on the steps and in the lanes of the garden surrounding the cathedral, family and friends become acquainted. They speak Russian, French, and English with sincere goodwill and a unanimous desire to be kind. The girls from the Red Cross are a great success. Everyone meeting them for the first time is impressed by their gaiety, and by how close they are to the newlyweds. The girls go from one group to the next to make sure that no one is feeling left out or alone. Every so often Mistou or Rolanne will slip away to run over and hug Claire. "Everybody's getting along so well!" they say, or, "What a splendid wedding!" Plumette, as section chief, is keeping an eye on everything. "A really classy show," she says approvingly, "a really classy show!" The weather is fine and warm, with the scent of lilacs everywhere; for a brief moment the French guests standing outside the cathedral Saint Alexander Nevsky feel as if they are in Russia. A Russia at peace, a country that has nothing to do with the Soviet Union—once again, people have been saying, altogether too often, that world peace is in danger.

While listening to the chatter of a former colonel in the White Army, Olga secretly observes the way Claire's parents are conversing with Wia's parents. The difference between the two couples is striking: Monsieur Mauriac and his wife are so elegant compared to the other couple in their shabbily tailored clothes. It is most striking in the women. Claire's mother is wearing a wide-brimmed rice-straw hat and a long gray silk dress that emphasizes her slender form and fine features. Wia's mother looks lumpy in a worn blue dress, and, in spite of the summer heat on this July day, she is wearing an ugly dark hat and an old fox fur around her neck. "Poor, dear Princess Sophie, she no longer knows how to dress or how to behave," thinks Olga sadly.

Berlin, July 12
Dear adorable little Mama,
I haven't written any sooner because the plane won't be leaving until tomorrow morning.

The drive went very well. We got up to 115 kilometers an hour and the car hardly shook at all. We took the top down as soon as we left the rue Raynouard. You can imagine our faces by the time we got to Berlin: roasted bright pink, etc.

Thank heaven, we found our room all ready for us in my former bedroom at number 96. You can imagine how pleased I was not to have to run to the other end of Berlin.

Absolutely tons and tons of flowers were waiting for me. You cannot imagine how kind everyone has been with me.

This evening there's going to be a big reception. I have to confess I'm not really looking forward to it. I'll have to stand at the entrance with Rosen and greet people. What a strange job!

In principle, Wia and I will be leaving tomorrow at around two o'clock.

My health isn't bad except for the occasional migraine, which comes and goes without a why or wherefore.

My dear sweet mother, I'll leave you now, sending all my love. I adore you and above all don't forget that I adore you more than anything on earth.

I'm so happy to be your daughter. I will try to be worthy of you.
A hundred thousand kisses, dear Mama.

July 13
We went to bed at four o'clock. It was quite extraordinary. There were generals from every country there. People had a lot to drink and they were pleased. We're leaving at two o'clock. I adore you.

Claire and Wia have hardly slept, they still have to do their packing, and there is an extraordinary upheaval in what used to be the floozies' room, which Mistou has now left. In the adjacent bathroom, Wia is shaving and whistling the *Internationale*, which he learned from his Soviet comrades. He got up first—Claire could not bring herself to leave the bed—and he was immediately in a good mood, in a hurry to leave, in a hurry to live. "Unbelievable, to have that sort of temperament," thinks Claire. She continues to be amazed that she is married to this man, this Russian, this "Martian," as she calls him. It makes her dreamy. Distractedly, she caresses Kitz, who is dozing at her feet, and she lights the first cigarette of the day, the best one.

"You smoke too much and too early."

Wia comes out of the bathroom. His hair is clean and well groomed, he is freshly shaven, and he smells sweetly of lavender eau de toilette. A glance out the window at the clear blue sky, and he turns back to Claire with a triumphant expression.

"What magnificent weather!"

"It's unbelievable—to be so happy, from the moment you wake up!"

"I'm happy because I love you, because you're my wife, and because we're going on our honeymoon."

In the July sunshine Claire and Wia discover a part of Germany where nature once again has the upper hand. Leaves are growing on trees they thought would be charred forever, meadows are lush and green, fields of wheat have been planted once again. The smallest villages have flowers hanging in abundance from the balconies. Claire often drives, and they go wherever their whim—and the convertible hired by their friends—takes them. They have a few visits planned, but they have also left room for improvisation, for a freedom that reminds them of their holidays before the war. They swim in lakes and rivers, climb hills, explore cool forests. "Germany has the most beautiful forests in the world," Claire likes to say. Wia takes pictures of Claire in her shorts, swimming suit, and summer dress. He wants to keep these moments of happiness forever.

On July 17, they are in Berchtesgaden, and from the balcony of their hotel, Claire takes several photographs of Hitler's Eagle's Nest.

Two days later, they are staying in the home of a German woman, a widow without children, who stopped supporting the Nazi regime when her husband was killed on the Russian front. She prepares a comfortable room and lends them a canoe, because her house is on the shore of a big lake that reflects the hills all around. She cooks for them, dishes they will not soon forget: these are the first fresh vegetables they've eaten in such a long time. She grows them in secret in a corner of her garden. And there is a Skye terrier that gave birth to a litter of six puppies, now three months old.

Stretched out in a meadow in the shade of an ancient fir tree, Claire and Wia talk about their friends in Berlin and their desire to see them again soon. In this gorgeous nature they have forgotten the four years of war and the threat of a new conflict between America and Soviet Russia. It is as if they were learning to live again.

"When we get back, we should leave again for a few days with the girls. There's no reason why they shouldn't have some vacation, too," suggests Wia.

"Good idea. In September, to enjoy the Indian summer? Where could we go?"

They feel wonderfully free, listing all the possible destinations.

The morning of their departure, their hostess presents them with one of the puppies, the one that Wia seems to prefer above all the others. And before they can protest, in the simplest German so that Claire will understand, she says: "This is a wedding gift to you, and a celebration of peace between our two countries. A commitment to the future . . . "

A few more days in the winter resort of Kitzbühel, then the cities of Salzburg and Munich, where Claire meets Wia's cousin Missie and her American husband, Peter. The two couples get along well and promise to meet often. The puppy goes everywhere with them, and Wia has decided to call him Vicouny: he will be their good luck charm.

Berlin, October 9, 1946

Dear Mama,

Why don't you ever write? I really do get the feeling that you have all completely forgotten me. Are you still in Malagar? How was the grape harvest this year? What is Papa doing? Etc., etc.

I intend to go to Paris toward the end of this month. Do you mind having me? You cannot imagine how happy I will be to see you all again. I get the impression I left you years and years ago, and it's been too long.

Life doesn't change here very much. After a horrible spell, the sky is clear again, but it's cold and we have had the heating on since yesterday.

Rosen is still in America and the house is fairly dreary and silent. Wia is working a great deal, particularly as this is France's month. My health is all right. The other day I had a fairly bad spell of indigestion, but I have to admit that I had deserved it.

Claire breaks off. Should she give her mother the details about why she had such a bad spell?

She and Wia, who are very popular with different Allied groups, had been invited to dinner by the Brits. Claire had initially refused, because she has always said she doesn't like the English, because they "burned Joan of Arc and poisoned Napoleon." Then she changed her mind: there was another grievance she had against their country, and she wanted to have it out with them.

The only woman at a table full of men, she had no qualms

about referring to the speech Churchill gave in March, 1946, at an American university, where he had used the now famous formula "the Iron Curtain." The surprised silence that greeted her opening words intimidated her. But Wia's confident gaze gave her the courage to go on, and after gulping down two whiskeys one after the other she stood up. Standing, looking down at all those men seated before her, she continued her argument.

When Churchill spoke of the Anglo-American alliance that would be necessary to fight communism in Europe, he had deliberately excluded France. This was humiliating and unfair. Had he forgotten General de Gaulle's appeal on June 18, the army of shadows, the resistance movements . . . When the British interrupted Claire with applause, she sat down. "I'm proud of you," whispered Wia, while a general got up in turn to propose a toast, in broken French, to "the *fitness* of the pretty Frenchwoman, the wife of my dearest Wia."

And after that? Claire doesn't remember very well what happened. Intoxicated with her success and the increasingly warm atmosphere around the table, she too had toasted to brotherhood between the British and the French. And she had not merely pretended to drink, as she had done with the Russians—she had drunk. Far less than all the men, to be sure, but enough to end up roaring drunk, standing on the table to raise a toast to Trafalgar, Nelson's brilliant victory over the combined fleets of the French and Spanish Navies.

Three days have gone by since that evening. "Dear Lord," thinks Claire, "I'm so ashamed . . . " Fortunately Wia had been understanding and even gallant: "Don't worry," he said the next morning when she finally woke up. "We were all a thousand times more drunk than you were and we've forgotten everything. But you have to promise me that from now on you will take care to remain sober."

No, Claire mustn't share this episode with her family. A

few caresses to her two dogs, who have been sick as well, and are fast asleep at her feet, a glass of water and a cigarette, and she can get back to her letter. She likes the calm, warm atmosphere in the bedroom when she's there without Wia; the way it used to be when Mistou was away.

I'm still fairly tired. I am feeling such nostalgia for the South of France and even for Malagar. The lack of smells here (I don't mean corpses) makes me want to weep with sadness. I can spend hours dreaming about mist, and sunshine, and the smell of grass fires, and everything you see in the month of September in Malagar. When I think that life is so short and that I'm not even living where I would like to be, well . . .

Yesterday I bought a lovely little accordion.

The other day we went to a Russian concert. The choirs were magnificent, but in my opinion all those young Russians, their faces illuminated with joy, were even more beautiful.

The other night I wore your evening gown. It looks lovely on me and despite the color it was the nicest one there. I must say the English and even the American women have the oddest way of dressing. They really are ugly and it makes you miss the days when only uniforms were allowed.

Dear little Mama, I have to go now, and I kiss you tenderly even though you are so naughty.

I hope to see you soon.

Six o'clock.

A letter, at last, it just arrived. I'm very glad to have it. You are so lucky to be at Malagar, and it's still lovely summery weather. I have the photograph before my eyes. And it's not the G. Duhamels, or even Claude or Papa that I've been looking at so eagerly, but the white wall with the shadows of those huge leaves I love so much.

Now since you asked, let's talk about me. I do indeed think I am expecting a child, but I'm not at all sure; that is why I didn't want to talk about it, and I beg you not to tell anyone. I've just started my second month without my period. If that's what it is, I have no cause for complaint because, although I always feel slightly queasy, I haven't really been downright nauseous. Nor have I put on any weight, except maybe in my breasts, which seem enormous and are fairly painful.

Naturally I'm being very careful. No sports, ambulance driving once in a blue moon when there's no one else. I'm so tired that I go to bed very early and get up very very late.

That's the only reason, you see, that I didn't dare go to Malagar. I was afraid of the trip. If you only knew how much I would have liked to. That's also why I decided to wait till the end of the month to go to Paris, because I think that will be the right time to see a doctor.

Having said that, I'm surprised not to feel more nauseous and maybe the child is just in my imagination.

I don't even know yet whether I'm really happy. For the moment it makes me desperate to have this body that fails to react to life: I don't feel like running, I don't feel like having fun. My body has no pep anymore, it's lifeless, I hardly recognize it, and I get the feeling it's dead, devoured by something unknown which is sucking everything from me whether I like it or not. And for the time being I am jealous of that unknown thing about to deform me, and I already hate the nine months ahead where I'm bound to lose myself perhaps never find myself again.

And then suddenly I see a little child and I'm mad with joy. Basically I lack imagination. I can't put a face or a soul to what I'm feeling at the moment.

And then where am I going to put this child? Where will we be in nine months? If I had my own house I would prepare for it with love. In three or four months, when I'll be dragging around like a monster, it will be impossible to stay here. I just can't see myself going up and down the stairs of number 96 in a uniform and a huge belly. Maybe I won't be so modest by then, but just the idea of it is enough to provoke a miscarriage. Where should I go?

I can't go invading you either with this big belly in front of me and then, above all, I need a place to put this big belly when it is fed up with being so big. And so, I need an apartment, too. I have no idea what it will cost. I would so like to have a place of my own, a place for expecting and welcoming a baby.

Enough for this evening. I'm sending you a big, big hug. Will you be happy to have a grandson?

Give everyone a big kiss for me, Papa, Claude, Jean, and Luce.

I'll be in touch very soon my Mama.

PS. I'm not used to my new name yet. Where did my adorable "Mauriac" go?

Two tearooms have opened not far from the Kurfürstendamm, and they are striving to give their customers an impression of luxury and comfort. Wia has chosen the one with a fireplace, where a lively fire is always burning, and there are windows with colored panes and a profusion of pastries. Pretty young *Berlinerinnen* in black dresses and white aprons ensure the service beneath the watchful eye of an older woman. They come and go among the tables, silent and smiling. Claire is fascinated by them, and has been somewhat neglectful of Wia's guest, his favorite cousin Tatiana, who married prince Paul von Metternich at the beginning of the war.

She's a tall, very beautiful woman, wrapped in a luxurious fur coat that she has not taken off despite the warmth of the room. She speaks incredibly quickly, in three or four languages, with the self-confidence of someone who is used to being listened to and admired. From time to time she glances at Claire as if to make sure she is still there, then she goes back to her descriptions of the restoration work she would like to have done at her castle at Johannisberg.

"Speak French," protests Wia, "you know that Claire only speaks French."

"I was saying that Johannisberg was destroyed in a bombardment in August, 1942. The fire trucks and the neighbors tried in vain to put out the huge blaze. All the inhabitants in Blingen on the far shore of the Rhine gathered to watch the tragedy. Many of them were crying, because Johannisberg was the pride of the entire province and even beyond, one of Germany's jewels."

Claire struggles to keep a sympathetic smile on her face while Wia asks his cousin to describe how they lived during the war. He remembers gratefully that she came to visit him when he was a prisoner. Claire thinks he is paying an awful lot of attention to her, and this reinforces the irritation she felt right from the start in Cousin Tatiana's presence. She annoys me with her castle, she is absolutely annoying, thinks Claire, lighting a cigarette. But Tatiana has already forgotten her and is speaking Russian again, punctuating her sentences with peals of laughter while she plays with her rings, her bracelets, and her long pearl necklace.

"I asked you to speak French," says Wia again.

"It doesn't matter," Claire hastens to say.

She is feeling more and more bored. She wonders if there is any way she can slip away and leave the two cousins alone to share their news and memories. Tatiana briefly fell silent after Claire's interruption but now she is looking at her with a sort of ill-humored curiosity. Then, taking a cheerful, worldly tone: "You really aren't very cosmopolitan, my dear."

"Not really, no."

"But you are determined to change, I suppose?"

"Not at all."

Claire adopts the expression of a sulky child. She pretends to be fascinated by some customers who have just come in, an American officer with a young German woman who is very thin and visibly famished. Tatiana makes a few remarks about the suffering of the defeated nation then turns to Claire with a protective, kindly manner.

"As Princess Wiazemsky, you will have to learn at least three languages. Russian is important first and foremost, because you will have to speak it to the children you are going to have. Isn't that right, Jim?"

On top of it, she's calling him by the nickname he used before the war, to exclude me from their world, thinks Claire, hesitating to reply.

Wia answers in her place.

"Claire has decided to learn Russian. She's starting this very week."

Tatiana beams a happy smile at the young couple, and begins to say something in German, apologizes, starts again in English and then bursts out laughing.

"I do apologize, my dear, but we are so used to going from one language to the next, quite fluently . . . And I imagine you must be very proud of becoming a princess, and that you are very determined to do honor to your rank? Or am I mistaken?"

"Claire couldn't care less about becoming a princess."

Tatiana is completely thrown by Wia's good-natured reply. To regain some of her formidable self-confidence she takes a compact and lipstick from her bag. Claire observes her moodily, because she thinks she knows what her husband's cousin must be thinking. "She suspects me of being a little bourgeoise who's got her hooks into a nobleman," Claire thinks. Claire would like nothing more than to get up and leave the tearoom without a word, or to find a way to make fun of Tatiana or deliberately spill her tea all over her fur coat. But then she sees Wia's trusting gaze and she thinks better of it.

Tatiana has finished reapplying her makeup. If Wia and Claire's words have shocked her, she's not letting it show.

"Claire is the daughter of a famous writer, François Mauriac," Wia declaims, proudly.

Tatiana does not let him continue, and she turns to Claire.

"Do you know that we also have writers in the family? My mother is just finishing up her memoirs, my sister Missie kept a remarkable journal until her marriage, and I also intend to write my memoirs at some point. Not to mention all the letters we have exchanged, which are very amusing!"

That evening at dinner Claire entertains her friends with an imitation of Cousin Tatiana's manners. She is not about to forget how humiliated she felt during their encounter at the tearoom, and she already knows she will never get over it. Never mind if Wia is upset.

"He can go all by himself to see her in her castle, that pretentious know-it-all!"

Instinctively, Claire places her hands on her belly. Her friends have not been informed yet. They are preparing the agenda for the next few days, and suddenly without warning Claire blurts out, "I have something to tell you, girls: it's unbelievable—I'm pregnant!"

October 18, 1946

Dear Papa and Mama,

There's a plane leaving soon. So I'm rushing to send you a few lines simply to tell you that I am now positive that if everything goes well I will be giving you a grandchild seven months from now.

Now that I know, I'm nearly crazy with joy and I don't care anymore about the big belly I'll have.

If it's a boy, his name will be François, and I hope, dear Papa, that you will agree to be his godfather.

Well now, as I have to hurry, I won't tell you any more today, other than that Wia is as happy as I am.

I send you absolutely huge hugs and kisses.

I'll be in touch soon.

The room Claire shares with Wia has been re-baptized "the newlyweds' room." There are photographs of their honeymoon tucked into the corners of the mirror or pinned up on the wall, waiting to be framed. There are no more items of clothing draped over the furniture, because Wia is very tidy. "And he polishes his boots himself every day!" Claire often says, admiringly.

In two weeks she will have to go to Paris for additional medical exams, and to see her family and have a rest. While she feels at home in Berlin, she often misses her family. She needs to see her father and mother, find out what her brothers are doing, and ask her sister about the ups and downs of pregnancy: Luce has already had two little girls and is pregnant again. Claire is sure that they are both going to have boys. "They'll be born two months apart," she thinks. She sits dreaming for hours on end about these two cousins: they'll meet during the summer vacations in Malagar, they'll grow up together and never be apart.

Berlin, December 2, 1946
Dear Mama,
Just a little note to let you know that we had a good trip despite being six hours late and a huge migraine that lasted twenty-four hours. I also broke my jar of cream which is very annoying.

Berlin is exactly as I left it. I was so happy to see my two dogs again, but Kitz is still coughing.

I've just come back from a big luncheon hosted by the Americans from Wia's division in honor of some old tradition where they eat goose. It was just as bad as can be. (Try and imagine what a goose cooked by Americans must taste like!) There were fifteen of us: all the Frenchmen, Americans, English, and Russians from the section.

It is unbelievable, the French are like the favorite children of the Americans, the English, and the Russians. One of them was a charming man from the Caucasus who said I looked so much like the girls from his country that he wants me to bring me a costume.

Everything is fine except the food here that I can hardly stand anymore. Yesterday during the day I felt so nauseous that I threw everything up. This morning I very nearly did the same.

I'm really unlucky, because the day before I arrived the water heaters burst. No more hot water and no more heating in my room. We got the water back this morning, but we won't have any heat for another two weeks or so.

Rosen isn't coming back until the twenty-third. This really annoys me: not for his sake, but for Wia's, because he's getting grouchier by the day. In spite of this, he's delighted with what he's doing. It's true that everyone adores him. The Russians treat him like royalty.

Dear Mama, I have to leave now but I thank you from the bottom of my heart for what you did for me, and Papa, too, while I was in Paris. I was really glad to spend time with you both the way we used to.

A very big hug to you and to Papa, too.

PS 1: Tell Papa that the American is delighted with his signed book.

PS 2: I will be thinking about Claude on Saturday and especially the other days. I'm very proud and I tell everyone that my brother is going to England to give lectures!

Rolanne refused to let Claire sit behind the wheel, and for once she's driving the ambulance. Claire didn't argue. Ever since she found out she was pregnant, she has been taking a few precautions: she no longer goes on very long expeditions, and she avoids traveling by car as much as she can. She feels useless, it puts her in a very bad mood, and she has complained about it to her companions. She also complains that she doesn't see enough of Wia: as long as he is replacing Rosen at the head of the Displaced Persons Section, he has to get up very early, and comes back very late.

But today is different.

The ambulance is transporting four men that the Soviets finally agreed to hand over to the Red Cross after some particularly lengthy negotiations: two Belgians, a Frenchman, and a young Greek.

Claire insisted on being there, for the sake of the young Greek. In all these months and years she has never felt such an intense need to save another person's life; never before has she tried so hard to make a case—first, to Wia, then, through him, to the authorities at the prison camp.

They hardly know a thing about this young kid, roughly eighteen years of age: he was captured by the Germans, then the Soviets considered him a collaborator, which meant he would be deported without a trial, with no one to argue his innocence. As they helped him lie down in the ambulance Claire and Rolanne immediately saw that he was in very bad shape, that he had tuberculosis. He had to be hospitalized at once. But where could they find room? All the hospitals in Berlin were full. "Let's try anyway," the two women decided together.

At the first hospital, they managed to find room for a few hours for the two Belgians and the Frenchman. But by the third hospital and another refusal they no longer knew what to do.

"Let's go back and see them one more time," Claire implored Rolanne. "You have to insist. You know how to bluff your way in several languages . . . Every minute counts if we want him to live."

"You're right."

Rolanne gives up on trying to park the ambulance properly, and climbs out after readjusting her coat and shapka. The day before, the temperature dropped below zero, and a layer of ice covers the ground. Claire stares dejectedly at all the buildings that are still in ruins in this neighborhood of Berlin, and she succumbs to a moment of despondency. She's expecting a child, but with her there is a young boy who is going to die and she feels helpless to save him. Is there really nothing to be done? She can stay by his side at least, so as not leave him alone with the fear of death.

She lifts the canvas tarp and climbs into the back of the ambulance. The young Greek is lying lifelessly on the bunk where they laid him. In spite of two military blankets he is trembling with cold and fever. His eyes are closed. But when he feels Claire's hand on his forehead, he suddenly opens his eyes and looks at her: a desperate gaze, pleading for help. "It will be all right, it will be all right," says Claire, stroking his face. In her simple gesture she puts all the delicacy she knows she is capable of when confronted with the misery of the world and the horrors of war. His huge, shining black eyes do not leave her face, and she would like to think that something of her lifeblood is reaching him. But the impression doesn't last, and he is soon trembling again convulsively.

"How stupid I am!" Claire takes off her coat and places it on top of the military blankets. Is it her imagination? It seems to her the boy is not trembling so badly now, and is avidly breathing in the perfume that lingers in the weave of the coat. "Après l'Ondée," she says. She begins to talk to him about Paris, about the cruise her family took to Greece before the war. She would say anything to keep that tiny flame of life in the boy's eyes.

He begins to speak in a low voice interrupted by violent fits of coughing. "No, be quiet, it's exhausting you." He obeys. Tears of pain, or despair, Claire isn't sure which, well in his eyes. Claire didn't understand what he was trying to say, but she thinks she has guessed. From their very first missions in the Soviet camps, Claire and her colleagues were surprised by the terror all these young men shared: "Don't let me die here," they would say. Meaning Berlin, Germany, far from home. "You're going to go back to Greece," murmurs Claire, who is not at all sure of this, but she wants to continue to breathe a bit of life into him.

Rolanne has been gone for over a quarter of an hour. Without her coat, Claire is beginning to feel very cold. But she goes on caressing the boy's face and hair, she goes on speaking to him. He has stopped crying, he seems to cling to her words, to the contact of her hand on his skin. Claire knows very well that he doesn't speak French, and that he can't understand her, but she goes on talking. She tells him that the Red Cross ambulances in Berlin were designed for the war in Libya, and that is why they only have canvas tarpaulins and are so cold.

"Before, during the war, the Red Cross had little Amilcars. You should have seen me at the wheel, I looked swell."

The boy's eyes close, he is no longer reacting to her words or caresses. Claire is frightened: this would not be the first time

162 · ANNE WIAZEMSKY

someone dies in her arms; she recognizes the signs. Then she hears Rolanne shouting her name and the sound of boots on the frozen ground near the car.

Back in the apartment, after a steaming bath to get warm again, Claire and Rolanne meet in the kitchen over a cup of tea. They try to convince themselves that the young Greek is out of danger and will get better. They refuse to believe the negative prognosis of the military doctor who hospitalized him.

"He'll pull through," says Claire stubbornly. "It's like a pledge, as if there in the back of the ambulance, and afterwards, he had promised me that together we would fight. Do you remember?"

"Yes, Clarinette."

No sooner had they lifted him out of the ambulance than the boy had regained consciousness, his eyes seeking Claire's. Then he had grabbed her hand with an unimaginable strength and wouldn't let go. All the way to his bed in an overcrowded ward Claire had gone on talking, saying any old thing, everything that went through her head, just to keep him conscious. She had promised to return the next day and the days that followed.

"It's so stupid to get attached like this to a kid you don't even know . . . If he doesn't pull through . . . "

"No, Clarinette, it's normal, and that's what makes it so painful sometimes."

December 22, 1946

Dear Mama,

I've heard it's very cold in Paris. Here for the last ten or fifteen days it's been hovering between -10 and -15. Other than the heating, which breaks down from time, to time we can't really complain. And are you all right, not too cold?

Nothing new at this end. Time goes by so quickly, it's disconcerting, but I can't complain about that either.

Let's talk about me since I think that's what you're interested in.

I'm getting on very well, into my fourth month. I haven't changed much since Paris and if you didn't know I was pregnant, you still couldn't tell. Other than this bad spell due to the dreary, bad diet I have here, I'm fine and almost never have migraines.

I think the usual pain had spread to my kidneys. It hurt so much I couldn't move. I have a massage every morning and now it's much better.

Now, dear Mama, I'd like to wish you a merry Christmas. I'm a bit sad to be away from you for the holiday. Rosen is leaving Paris this evening. We already have four Christmas trees in the house and I think we'll have a very nice celebration.

Wia has told me to kiss you very tenderly. He is presently head of the section and is having a grand time playing the Important Man.

Once again, Merry Christmas my adorable Mama.

Your little Claire.

December 30, 1946

Dear Mama,

Happy New Year! Naturally this letter will reach you too late, but I've had a bout of flu these last few days and didn't have the strength to pick up my pen. I hope you had a good Christmas and that you'll have a good New Year's Day.

It's exactly a year ago today that you met Wia for the first time. I had just arrived in Paris, with two long months to spend with you. Now I don't know when I'll be able to come and see you. I don't even know if Wia will take any vacation. He has a lot of work and doesn't want someone to fill in for him or even help him. He likes being indispensable. Basically if that's what he likes, too bad for him. But he doesn't look well, he's losing his hair and aging before my very eyes. In spite of that, he is absolutely adorable and we never argue.

Apart from the flu I'm in good health. I put on a terrible amount of weight practically overnight. I don't know if you recall the etching in grandmother's big Bible that was on the table at the end of the drawing room. It showed Samson with one hand on each column of the temple that was collapsing under the pressure. I get the same impression. As if the child were pushing on all sides and everything cracking inside me. I think he's going to be very strong because I am hard and tough and he is having a difficult time finding his place. He's also hellishly high-strung, so at any rate he will be a son worthy of his father.

I am really lucky with the life I'm leading at the moment. I don't know what I would do if I had to work. Just imagine, this morning I had breakfast in bed and then after a good massage I had a lovely bath. I can't say I'm having huge amounts of fun but who is having fun? I tire very quickly and the least little outing is a real drama. Speaking of outings, I've just thought of the jacket. It's a nice green color but what can I wear it with? In fact I think I need something I can wear in the evening and what could I wear under the green? By the way, I hope you've been using my fur coat while the weather's been so cold.

My adorable Mama, I kiss you with all my heart and I wish you and Papa a very very happy New Year.
Your little Claire.

Glasses, empty bottles, and plates scattered here and there on the various floors of 96 Kurfürstendamm: all that's left of New Year's Eve, December 31, 1946, when the French were host to a number of American, British, and Russian Allied officers. As Claire wrote to her parents, her fellow residents are pleased to know how much they are appreciated, and glad too that collaborationist France has been forgotten for the sake of another France, a country that woke up again one morning after the war was over, the France they have found here in Berlin. For one night, Americans and Russians were friends again. They'd put aside the ever more threatening possibility of a new war between the two superpowers.

Everyone has woken up rather late on this morning of January 1, 1947. Rolanne and Plumette are having breakfast in the kitchen. They haven't woken Mistou, who was last to bed, after being crowned "Queen of the party" and dancing until dawn and sheer exhaustion.

Claire has just joined them but she still feels dozy. She was a great hit with her accordion, and she persuaded her comrades from the building and their guests to sing in every language. She had rehearsed in secret, and her progress surprised everyone.

"We didn't realize: you are quite the musician," says Rolanne.

"You'd be good for the Army shows," adds Plumette.

"For the Americans? With my huge stomach? Absolutely not!"

Wia bursts into the kitchen, followed by the two dogs. "Let's have a look at that huge stomach!"

He's already been for a ride on his favorite horse, and his face is red from the cold, the speed, and the joy of living. He has the day off, for the first time in a long while, and he has every intention of taking advantage of it. Claire pretends to protest.

"It's unbelievable, how can you be so fit after all you drank last night!"

But she gets up off her chair, pulls on her boots and her fur-lined coat, and tugs the shapka down to her eyebrows: it is -15 again today, she checked the thermometer hanging outside the kitchen window. Just then Léon de Rosen comes in. He, too, has been up for a long time, he has even started on his round of New Year's wishes to the various members of his managing committee.

"Happy New Year, all of you! By the way, Claire, your little protégé, the Greek chap, had a good night. It looks like he's going to make it."

Claire and Wia set off for a walk in the park nearby. There is a thick layer of ice and they move slowly, for fear of slipping. The dogs run far ahead, constantly sliding. They delight a small group of children wearing old-fashioned ice skates who have turned a little pond into their private skating rink. The air is dry and brisk, a pale sun breaking through the clouds now and again. Sometimes Claire and Wia walk past other couples, Berliners who wish them a happy New Year in German. Small clouds of vapor form as they speak.

"My little Greek has been saved and these children have forgotten there was a war. My son will be born into a better world," says Claire joyfully.

"What makes you think it will be a boy? A girl would be nice, too . . . "

"It will be a boy. François will be born in May, and—"

Wia interrupts her with a kiss.

"I forgot to tell you. I was able to speak to my father on the phone yesterday. He's asked us to respect our two countries of origin and to choose names accordingly."

"What do you mean?"

"You know. No François if it's a boy, no Frances if it's a girl, but names that can be shared by France and Russia, like Leo, Alex, Peter, Serge, John, Marie, Anne, Helen, Natalie, etc.. There are plenty of names to choose from."

Claire stops in her tracks, seized by a sudden violent annoyance.

"Let's head back," she says, "I'm tired."

Wia did not notice his wife's change of tone and agrees goodheartedly. He whistles to call the dogs, the way he usually does. To his great surprise, neither one of them responds to his call. He waits for a few seconds, looking closely at the area of the park where he last saw them, imagines they must be playing with the children, and whistles again, louder and longer. A few more seconds go by and he sees Kitz in the distance, bounding out of a tangle of dead trees strewn across the ground. Kitz is all alone; there is no sign of Vicouny.

For three hours Claire and Wia called their dog, looking everywhere. The children helped them, and then a few unknown German volunteers joined in, and they searched every corner of the park and all the neighboring streets. Kitz trotted alongside, looking sheepish. Several times over, Wia took him to one side and asked him what had happened to his companion. "He was your responsibility!" Claire hasn't the heart to protest against his absurd behavior. She shares her husband's distress, and does not realize that she is in fact exhausted, walking in the cold like this. Fog has settled over the city, making it harder to search.

Finally they decide to go home.

It's January 1, a holiday, and there are not many people

upstairs in the Displaced Persons Section. But the girls from the French and Belgian Red Cross are nearly all there. Plumette immediately comes forward to take charge of the operations. Wia, Mistou, and three of their Belgian comrades, each of them at the wheel of a car, set off to patrol the streets of Berlin. Claire and Rolanne stay at home to welcome Vicouny in case someone, miraculously, brings him back.

Wia and their friends do not return until well after dark. They questioned everyone they met, fearing the worst: in Berlin they have lost count of the number of dogs and cats stolen either to be sold to the highest bidder or eaten by the most famished.

Claire worries that her husband is about to lose his mind. She suggests they put up a notice with a huge reward for whoever happens to find him. "In every language," she insists, "in every language." Wia sets to work at once, with the girls' help. They all pretend not to notice that he is weeping profusely.

> January 6, 1947
> Mama,
> Just a quick note to tell you that everything is fine; Rolanne will be taking the train in a few minutes. I'll write a longer letter very son.
> I thought about you all a lot on New Year's Day and this morning I took communion for you and Papa (some of it was for my son as well).
> I am sure you must have spent a better first of January than Wia and I did, because we lost our dog Vicouny, and spent two days looking everywhere for him. Thanks to the huge reward that we promised, he was brought back on the second in the evening. But I'll tell you all about it another time.

Claire stops writing. No, she won't say another word about how Wia behaved when Vicouny disappeared; such insane love . . . Her parents would never even begin to understand how anyone can become so attached to an animal. She herself no longer knows what to think. She suspects she will never forget those hours of anxiety, the question she asked herself and still asks: Will Wia be able to show greater love for his son than for his dog? She remembers how brutally he chased Kitz from their bedroom to punish him for not keeping better watch over Vicouny. Kitz sought refuge in Mistou's room and is still there. And again she sees Hilde, their occasional translator, informing them that Vicouny had been found at last; and the enormous amount of money the person who had "taken him in," so to speak, was asking.

But Rolanne's voice in the stairway puts an end to her ruminations.

"I'm leaving!"

Claire has to finish her letter.

In a gilded wooden frame there is a photograph of Claire on her knees in the middle of a meadow with Vicouny in her arms. The tall grass, the wildflowers, the clear light, her little frock and the happy smile on her face all evoke summer and carefree happiness. Wia took the photograph on the last day of their honeymoon, a dozen miles or so from Berlin. Other photographs show her wearing shorts or a swimsuit. Claire looks at them with a mixture of pride and sorrow. It seems that only now has she realized how pretty she was then, how slim and elegant. Will she ever be that young woman again? She has her doubts. There is one last photograph where she is standing among the Red Cross girls, dated December 31, 1946: her heart sinks. She looks bloated, old. "My son, my son, this is just too much, you're wearing me out," she says. Lately whenever she is alone she catches herself talking to him with a mixture of reproach and encouragement, words of love, surprising words, that come to her from deep inside.

Claire is annoyed when she remembers she has an appointment to meet Hilde. As her comrades are on the road, it is "the

German woman," as she calls her, who will drive her to the hospital where the young Greek is being treated. Unlike Rolanne, Claire is curiously mistrustful of Hilde. Worse yet— she is willing to bet that Hilde was in some way responsible for Vicouny's disappearance and the sum of money they had to pay to get him back.

B erlin, January 14
Dear Mama,
Wia is out at a dinner party he was obliged to attend, so I'm
writing to you from my bed. It's already well past eleven.

Today you could almost feel the spring in the air: everything
was melting, and it was beautiful. Water dripping everywhere,
and that precious smell of springtime. Naturally I was the only
one here who noticed. I know that Jean would have come home
and said, "It's marvelous, it's like spring," but he wasn't here so I
was the only one who enjoyed it. Four days ago it was still -23, the
day before yesterday -20, yesterday it was snowing and today it's
springtime. The cold was terrible but I didn't notice it all that
much because I didn't go out very often. But the Berliners must
have really suffered from it.

Thank you for your letter, which I finally got this morning! It's
strange because only yesterday I was saying to Wia, "We're going
to have to decide at some point where to have the birth, because
Papa and Mama must be finding me rather neglectful."

Rosen has just come back from Paris. I haven't been able to
have a serious talk with him yet. But I think there are ninety-nine
chances out of a hundred that we will still be here in May. In a few
days I'll know if conditions are suitable to have the baby here. If
so, my son will be born in Berlin. Never mind! In Paris, I think I
would be in your way for at least two months because I couldn't
possibly show up one evening and leave again the next day. And
just imagine how much trouble it would be for you and Papa. It
will be so much simpler for you simply to get a telephone call.

Besides, a pregnant woman is not a pretty sight, still less a
pregnant woman who's giving birth. I would like so much to look
my best for you and Papa and my brothers, with a child in my

arms and a flat stomach. Having said that, I may be obliged to make you stay up all night. Let's hope not!

I'd be ever so grateful if you could buy everything I still need for the baby.

These days I've been fairly tired with terrible stomach cramps during the night. I don't think it's anything but tomorrow evening I'll have the results of the analysis and after that I'll go to see a doctor. The baby's growing very very slowly but surely. I get the impression he's having trouble finding his place, but fortunately he's stronger than my poor belly.

There is something I dream of doing, I feel almost sick I want it so badly: to run along a beach in the middle of summer and feel that my body is my own, all mine, then throw myself in the water, and relax, and get tired, and feel myself again!

It's terrible, I hardly think about the baby, and I don't love him yet.

Wia just stayed ten days all alone in charge of the section, with extraordinary sessions to prepare the conference in Moscow. He's gotten rather skinny and he's not looking his best but he's pleased with his work. He's often in a foul mood, but he reserves it for other people because with me he's adorable.

He's been making all the secretaries cry one after the other and he shouts at the rest of the section. The dogs and I are the only ones who enjoy his favor. And yet in spite of it all everyone here adores him.

I have to go now, sending kisses with all my heart and to Papa too, naturally.

Your little girl who loves you.

PS: It was impossible to ring you on January 1, the line was only for big shots and emergencies.

The letter from my little Greek is adorable.

Claire looks tenderly at a group photograph taken a week ago. She is holding the arm of a thin young man who is leaning on crutches and staring at her adoringly. Plumette, Rolanne, and Mistou are standing on either side. It's snowing, they look like they're freezing. In the background you can just see the ambulance that is about to drive the young Greek to the airport. Thanks to the letter that he managed to send her, Claire now knows that he has been given a spot in a hospital in The Hague where they hope to cure his tuberculosis.

Berlin, January 24, 1947

Dear Mama,

Just a short note because there's someone taking the train in a very short while. Forgive me if this letter is only practical.

I went to the doctor I had seen already: he found me in very good shape. According to him, the baby should arrive on May 12 (but why the twelfth! I think it will be between the fifteenth and the nineteenth). I think I'll arrange to have the birth in a clinic run by nuns that looks very good. My tests have all come back fine.

There are heaps of things to do just now and I apologize.

1. Did anyone call to tell you that I thought the yellow jacket was very pretty? Particularly as the seamstress didn't make it too tight.

2. I'm sending you the prescription from Dr. P. Could you ring him and ask if it has to be refilled or changed? Would you be so good as to buy what is needed and get it to me by the person who is going to phone you?

3. I need some yarn, white if possible, 4 ply and 3 ply. Here they've only got 5 ply. And if I could have some knitting needles.

Poor poor Mama, if you only knew how sorry I am to bother you with this.

Thank you so much for the apples and endives (we made the most marvelous salad, the first since Paris) and the sugar. You're a dear.

I'd like to have the skirt from my black suit to go with the yellow jacket.

I think that's it.

I hope you're all fine. It's snowing here.

Yesterday evening I went to see *Rigoletto*. The singing was amazing, and I thought it was very very beautiful.

I haven't written back to Claude yet; he sent me such a kind letter. I'm so ashamed I don't know what to say. Or to Luce, although I think about her and her son every day.

Dear Mama, I'm sending you my warmest kisses.

Claire is about to slip the letter into the envelope when Wia comes into the room.

"Are you writing to your mother? Let me add a few words."

He sits down at the inlaid desk, which suddenly seems very small. "It's a desk for a young girl," thinks Claire dreamily. Despite the months that have gone by, she has not gotten used to her new name or her husband. And the thought that she will soon be the mother of a son is such a strange prospect that she cannot quite grasp it.

Wia is in a great hurry and writes quickly, his handwriting looping and legible.

> Most feared and beloved Maman,
> You must think I am a very nasty sort, forgetful and ungrateful. That's not the case at all! Your son-in-law is adorable and kind, and he is ever so fond of you (although he is still somewhat frightened, too, especially from a distance) but the poor man has had so much to do. He's a one-man orchestra, replacing in succession and often simultaneously nearly all the members of his section, from the orderly to the big chief. The poor fellow leaves his office at eight o'clock in the evening and only rarely is he not disturbed at least two or three times more after that. He has to see his beloved wife, and walk the dogs, and have dinner, and read the newspaper so that he doesn't entirely lose touch with the outside world (incidentally, bless you for the *Figaro* which gets here like a regular little express train, hardly three days old, which is incredible!).
> As a result, the days go by and I haven't had a minute for my personal life.
> In a few days I'll be leaving for five days in Denmark, unfortunately on an extremely official mission, so without Claire. Such a great pity!
> I kiss you with affectionate respect and ask you to forgive me once again for my long silence.

"Will that do?"

Claire rereads the letter very quickly.

"It will do. Anyway, you know you have completely charmed Mama."

Wia takes the envelope. In the doorway, he stops briefly to turn and look at this woman he loves so much, his wife, the mother of their child to come. He would like to thank her for being there, for being so pretty, and for choosing him over all those other men (or so he thinks). But he is afraid he will irritate her so he says something quite different. "I just heard that one of my best friends from before the war is on his way through Berlin. We took our final exams together. You will like him a lot, his name is Minko."

"Minko!"

Claire is so stunned that she drops the book she had just picked up. The dogs are startled, Wia comes back into the room and closes the door.

"You know Minko? That old charmer Minko?"

Claire suddenly feels incredibly happy. So her friend from long ago, whom she'd had no news of and had almost forgotten, is alive! She doesn't even notice how worried her husband has suddenly become, how lost and unhappy he looks. She is overjoyed to be talking about the past, telling Wia how she and Minko met in Paris when they were young, before the war; and how they met again on the Eastern front at the end of 1944; and the risks she had taken by going back to Paris without an official leave in order to find him the ambulance he needed. Wia is listening, perhaps more intently than he has ever listened to her before. For the first time he is filled with doubt about himself, about Claire's love. He suddenly imagines that she might leave him, just like that, from one day to the next, because this lover from her youth has reappeared.

"And how do you know Minko?"

How natural her voice is, her question is so simple. The horrible vision dissolves.

"Through the Alsatian school. We were a small group of

friends with foreign backgrounds. Namely, myself the Russian, Minko the Pole, and Stefan Hessel the German. It was a great place, the Alsatian school. They didn't look on us as foreigners but rather as international students. For the three of us, that was a very important distinction . . . "

Lost in the pleasure of telling Claire about that happy time, Wia forgets all about the scare he had a few minutes earlier. He tells her about their vacation in Spain, their canoe trip down the Ebro through Navarra, Aragon and Catalonia.

"I have never heard another word from Stefan and there is every reason to be worried . . . I hope that Minko will know what became of him. Of the three of us, Stefan Hessel was the most gifted for happiness and—"

Claire interrupts him with a gesture.

"The mail! We forgot to give them the mail!"

"Your mother will wait."

Rolanne has just come back from two weeks with her family, and has brought fruit and vegetables and mail for her comrades. For Claire there are letters from her brothers and sister and mother. They have all agreed that the right thing to do is give her child a name shared by France and Russia. They suggest Pierre, Natasha, or Andrei because of *War and Peace*, one of François Mauriac's favorite novels. "It will be Pierre, Petrushka," decides Claire.

She and Rolanne are walking briskly up the Kurfürstendamm, headed for the birth clinic: it is time for Claire to register. They have an appointment with Hilde who, once again, will act as interpreter to help Claire fill out the forms.

The beginning of April was rainy, but now the cold has returned to remind everyone that the terrible winter of 1946-1947 is not over, at least not for the German population. Because the country is still in ruins, and everything is in short supply: food, housing, clothing. Despite the ongoing use of ration cards imposed by the Allies, and since the summer, the UN aid packets, the population is still suffering from hunger, something that is apparent to Claire and Rolanne as they wander through the streets of Berlin.

Wretched-looking men and women continue to search through the rubble, most of the time without the help of any machines, with only their bare hands. Long ago they exchanged anything they still had for a bit of food from the countryside, and they would agree to any kind of work just to eat. Many of them are still living in cellars.

"You get the impression that nothing has changed for them," sighs Rolanne, "that they are still living in the 'zero hour,' the *Stunde Null*, as Hilde calls it."

Claire doesn't know what to say. Since she stopped driving the ambulance, she has been living with a vague sense of guilt. Even though she eats badly, and it is never quite what she would like, she is aware that she is enjoying enormous privileges. This bothers her with regard to the German women who are working for her now that she is pregnant. There's one who gives her a massage every morning, and another who will be looking after her child. Not to mention the women who come every day to do the cleaning throughout the building.

Hilde is waiting outside the partially rebuilt clinic. As always, she is wearing a large man's coat cinched at the waist with a military belt, and a beret pulled down low on her head. With her hands in her pockets and not a trace of emotion she watches as Claire and Rolanne come toward her.

"The papers are ready. All you have to do is dictate your answers to me, then sign them. Then you will have to come back with the money," she says in a neutral voice.

Claire and Rolanne follow her through a succession of rooms, minimally furnished but very clean. They see nuns and pregnant German women, who all turn around and stare as they go by.

"It's your Red Cross uniform," explains Hilde. "There are no foreigners here, not a single one."

She points to some chairs. While Claire and Rolanne sit down, Hilde looks frankly at Claire for the first time.

"Why have you decided to give birth in a German clinic?" she says abruptly.

"Because I've heard that the American doctors are dreadful, and I don't want to be chopped to bits!"

Claire had been briefly astonished by Hilde's unexpected curiosity and she hoped that her snap reply and sardonic smile would put an end to the conversation. But Hilde's smile in return is even more sardonic, a smile at the limits of insolence.

"And what do you know about your German doctor?"

"That he is the best one, that all the German women who have the choice ask for him."

"And what else? Haven't you wondered what he did during the war? Where he was? What his rank in the army was?"

Claire feels a sudden fright at the way Hilde is insisting with her questions. She has a gut feeling, almost a certainty, that Hilde is not beyond hurting her, that the child she is carrying and she herself might be in danger. Claire is overwhelmed by an animal desire to flee, to leave the clinic as quickly as possible, but she represses it.

"What are you insinuating?"

Is she the one being aggressive now? Hilde's face is once again neutral and indifferent.

"I'm not insinuating anything. He's an excellent doctor, your child will be born in the best conditions. You see, as the losers, we are no longer used to seeing the victors turn to us for our skills, that's all."

Hilde gets up from her chair and her legs suddenly crumple beneath her. It is only Rolanne's quick reaction that keeps her from falling to the tiled floor of the waiting room.

"It's nothing, it's the hunger."

"This time you will do as I say and come and eat something at our house," decides Rolanne.

A few hours later, the three women are sitting at the table in the kitchen. Rolanne is heating up some potatoes with lard; Hilde seems to devour the pan with her furtive gaze. Despite the warmth in the room she refuses to take off her coat or her beret. Claire would have liked to go back to her room but she has agreed to Rolanne's hushed request to keep them company. She places her hands on her belly, and follows the baby's disordered movement; he is now almost eight months old, and Claire has managed to stay so slim that you can hardly tell he is there. "You're so nervous, my son, you're wearing me out," she murmurs. She feels slightly nauseous, something Hilde's voracious appetite does not help: Rolanne has poured her a glass of whiskey and is encouraging her to drink and eat even more.

At last Hilde seems to have eaten her fill.

"This is my first real meal in so long, thank you," she says, preparing to stand up.

"Stay a while longer, tell us about yourself."

Hilde shrugs her shoulders but seems receptive to Rolanne's kindness, to her simple invitation. She looks at her for a moment as if to gauge the sincerity of her attentions, then she looks at Claire, totally absorbed in stroking her tummy.

The daylight fades from the kitchen, and Hilde is still talking. She tells them about the fall of Berlin and the Soviet occupation; famine, death, rape; how lucky she is to have survived and not gone mad like so many others. She tells them about the return of their men, how they refused to acknowledge the hell that their women have endured; the silence that has now been imposed upon the women of Berlin; how they are being forced to forget. She expresses herself without the slightest sentimentality, without complaining, without hatred, as if she were talking not about herself but a stranger. Rolanne and Claire listen in silence without interrupting. They know that it is all true. They instinctively understand that they must not express compassion, at the risk of hurting her, perhaps humiliating her. Finally Hilde falls silent.

"And now, what do you plan to do?" asks Rolanne.

"What do you think? Survive, save up some money, and leave."

There is a sound of yapping and a clatter of feet in the stairway, then light from the ceiling brutally floods the room as Wia bursts into the kitchen with the two dogs.

"Good God, why were you sitting here in the dark?"

Hilde immediately gets to her feet to take her leave. Wia notices her and bows, the old-fashioned gallantry he displays toward all women. Hilde merely gives a slight nod of her head, then disappears down the stairs, without looking at Claire or Rolanne.

"What a strange girl," says Wia. "Is she the one who works with you sometimes?"

Without waiting for their answer he says, "Go ahead with supper, I'm going to be late. Can you look after the dogs? Rosen doesn't want them in the office anymore."

Alone again, Claire and Rolanne sit on in silence as if to rest and find their footing in reality, their own reality, one that has nothing to do with Hilde's. Her presence seems to haunt the room.

"Brrr . . . I hope she hasn't brought my son bad luck," murmurs Claire finally.

Rolanne is shocked.

"Oh, Claire!"

"Now that I know her story better, I'm convinced she had something to do with Vicouny's disappearance and ransom. And you know what?"

Claire pauses for a second, then strikes a dramatic pose: "I'm not angry with her anymore."

Claire looks tenderly at the stout little woman bustling around her kitchen, and she feels protective toward her: there is no overt danger, she just wants to guard her from misfortune. She senses she is weak and vulnerable. The fact that she is Wia's mother never ceases to surprise her. There is absolutely no resemblance between her dashing husband and this weary, prematurely aged woman, between his extroverted personality and her deliberate self-effacement. But Claire began to love her almost immediately.

And yet it had not been easy: only a week ago, when Wia announced to her that his mother was arriving to spend a few days in Berlin and that she would be staying with them, Claire was shocked that he had not asked her for her opinion beforehand. Moreover, Wia already knew he would not have time to look after his mother. "This way you'll get to know one another," he said, nonchalantly.

Claire's sulking hostility had not lasted long. Her mother-in-law was so shy, and so sweet with everyone, and did everything she could to be pleasant to Claire. She constantly asked how she felt, how she had slept, and spoke lovingly about the baby's imminent arrival. She seemed to constantly forget her own self and thought only of others. She never complained, never spoke about her past life in Russia, or the hardship of these last twenty years in exile. For Claire and for her comrades, "Princess Sophie," as they affectionately referred to her, was the incarnation of goodness.

"Don't stay on your feet, *Dushka,* you'll get tired."

To please her, Claire sits down at the kitchen table.

"Would you like me to help you pack your suitcase?"

"In your condition?"

"I am fine, and if Petrushka were a little less agitated, I'd feel even better."

Before she has even had time to realize that she is thirsty, her mother-in-law has already poured her a cup of tea. Claire likes being spoiled and she appreciates the gesture. She asks Sophie to sit down beside her, which she does, gazing at Claire with a smile as she removes one of her earrings, a heavy opal set with little amethysts.

"No," says Claire firmly.

Since she arrived, her mother-in-law has not stopped giving her the few pieces of jewelry she still has left and which she wears every day. In Wia's harsh opinion, it makes her look like a Christmas tree. Claire has noticed that he is often very critical of his mother. How can he be so admiring with Claire, and yet at times so unkind toward others?

Mistou joins them in the kitchen, her hair tousled, exuberantly happy.

"I have leave to go to Paris. I'll be taking the same train as you, Princess Sophie. We'll have a marvelous trip, it's spring everywhere!"

"Mistou has gotten engaged," Claire explains to her mother-in-law.

There is a thick crowd on the station platform. Wia climbs into the carriage where the two women have their reservation, and helps his mother and Mistou settle in. As always, the train for Paris is packed, and many passengers will have to stand.

Claire is waiting on the platform, jostled here and there by the crowd. She wishes her husband would hurry, and take her home. Knowing she's so close to her due date tires and worries her. It is as if the child she is carrying—she insists on calling him Petrushka—were sapping all her strength. It's very hot for early May; this summertime heat makes her even more tired.

But now Wia is at her side, pointing to the window of the carriage where Mistou and his mother are standing. They are waving and blowing kisses. Claire finds the difference striking, between Mistou's triumphant youth and the older woman's resigned weariness.

"Your mother looks so sad," she says.

Wia puts a protective arm around her shoulders. He guides her firmly toward the way out, mindful no one bumps into them.

"I hope your father will be waiting at the Gare de l'Est and that he'll be glad to see her," insists Claire.

"My father has his own life, I'm not sure he'll be there."

"What do you mean?"

"Horses, shopping, friends, women, who knows . . . after that many years of marriage . . . "

In spite of the heat Claire suddenly feels chilled to the bone. She is horrified by his cruel words, his casual delivery. For a split second she sees their future, a future so dark that she is on the verge of feeling ill. She falters and Wia tightens his hold, kissing her tenderly on the brow.

That's their life. My life with Wia will be nothing like that, decides Claire.

The windows are open wide and the warm air drifts in, redolent of springtime. Will there soon be smells in the ruined city besides those of war and death? The perfume of trees and flowers, the perfume of life? Berlin's rebirth is so important to Claire: this is her adoptive city, it will be her son's city. She gazes in the mirror at her misshapen body and once again she is glad she will be giving birth far away from her family: this way at least they won't have to see the monster she thinks she has become. She has just written a teasing letter to her sister Luce, boasting that she will be the first to give birth to a grandson for their father. It is not for Wia's sake that Claire wants a son, but for her father's: she admires him more than anyone on earth, and she knows that he is hoping it will be a boy. Of course he won't have the beautiful name Mauriac, Papa, but Petrushka will be your first grandson. At least for once I'll beat my brothers and sisters to it! thinks Claire, with childish pride.

At the end of the day, Wia comes into the bedroom for a moment. He has brought her a fragrant branch of lilac with some foliage, and a letter he has just written to his mother-in-law. As usual, he would like Claire to read it.

She skims over what he has written about the increasingly tense relations between East and West—what he now calls the Cold War—to linger over one passage that is about her.

> Through Claire, I can share in your life, your joys and concerns: through her you know everything that is going on here, how we spend our time, our plans. Through me you will only learn the things that Claire does not tell you, such as the fact that she is more and more adorable (and adored) with each passing day. Because of this I often forget to tell her things about my work or how I spent my day, because I so often have the impression she has been at my side the whole time. She is never absent from my life, it is as if she were a part of me, and yet I am constantly discovering new things that makes me love her even more.
>
> My mother has left. I only saw her in the evenings and usually there were other people around, because we've had so many meetings at our house. Claire, on the other hand, spent most of her days alone with my mother, just the two of them, and you cannot imagine how adorably kind she was in every respect. My mother left in excellent physical and mental health—happy, rested, calm, and delighted with her stay, all thanks to Claire, and Claire alone.

Out of modesty, Claire turned to one side to hide her emotion upon reading the letter. She knows that she is loved, but a part of her still doubts, and will always doubt. Wia misinterprets her pensiveness, and says worriedly: "Is something wrong? Am I boring?"

Claire collects herself, hiding with a serious air her sudden desire to laugh: "No, Wia, no. But all the same, when you write to Mama . . ."

She hunts for the passage she had in mind, finds it and reads:

> Vicouny is the same as ever, that is, the perfect dog (for Claire and me) or a total imbecile (for the rest of mankind). He follows Claire wherever she goes and he adores her (how could he not?). That is, more or less, the news from the family.

"So?"

"So, it's unbelievable, you just don't realize that Mama doesn't give a fig about Vicouny!"

The birth did not go well. The infant breathed too soon and choked on its own breath; it owes its life exclusively to the doctor's know-how. Claire, half conscious, is in great pain. She has not slept for over twenty-four hours, and she is exhausted. When they tell her the infant has been saved and that it's a little girl who is now in perfect health, she refuses to see her. "All that, and for what!" she protests, turning her back and sinking into a deep sleep.

When she awakes, the light of the setting sun is filling the room. Through the windows she can see the branches of the linden tree tossing in the breeze. On her night table there is a bouquet of flowers, and at the foot of her bed there is a cradle. Then she remembers, she has given birth to a little girl, but the cradle is empty. She's filled with panic: what if the baby who had such trouble coming into the world has not survived? She looks for a bell, anything, so she can call for help.

Then the door opens and Wia comes in, holding the baby in his arms, and followed by Olga and Rolanne. All three of them are as radiant as they are touched. They all start talking at once, a confused chatter; they have been reassured and are wild with joy. All the residents of number 96 are waiting impatiently to come and embrace Claire. She wishes she could tell them to stop being so noisy and restless.

"Tomorrow, or the day after at the latest, I will introduce my daughter to all our friends," says Wia. "Take a closer look: a real muzhik!"

He holds the baby out to her but Claire, ill-tempered, refuses to hold her.

Distraught, Wia turns to Olga and Rolanne: what should he do with this woman, his wife, who has only been a mother for a few hours? Rolanne shrugs her shoulders cheerfully as if to suggest it's not important; he must give Claire time to get used to the idea. Rolanne holds the baby to her chest, rocking her, tickling her, humming the opening bars of a nursery rhyme. Olga is delighted by the baby's little cooing noises.

"Let me have her," she asks.

"No, she's my Berlin child."

Rolanne, holding the baby, is dancing around the bed, as if to show the baby how much joy she has brought into the world. "My Berlin child, my Berlin child," she chants. Wia sits down next to Claire. He takes her hands and tells her about the telephone calls with their two families—everyone sends their congratulations, and there are telegrams beginning to arrive from all over.

But Claire is hardly listening. With a mixture of irritation and stupor she watches as Rolanne twirls around the room, while Olga tries to coax the baby from her. Finally Claire's exasperation gets the better of her.

"Give me back my baby, my Berlin child."

Rolanne complies immediately. Claire, afraid at first, then with a touch more confidence, nestles the child in the hollow of her shoulder. How can it be that the infant lets her do this, without crying—look how trusting it is, content, even. Claire is beginning to realize, with some confusion, that this child comes from her, belongs to her. She is naively, sincerely surprised that she has been able to produce this little human being.

"It's unbelievable," she murmurs.

She caresses the infant's skin and cheeks, so soft, so tender, and sees that she does indeed have two hands and two feet; she is astonished by the baby's smiles, the little chirping sounds that come from her lips. Claire now feels so sure that the child is where it ought to be that she is overwhelmed by a wave of love and gratitude. She fails to notice the silence around her, how attentively Wia, Rolanne, and Olga are watching her every gesture.

"My Berlin child," she murmurs again.

Cautiously, timidly, she kisses the tiny hands, the brow, the golden down on her head. And suddenly, with a mixture of humor and reproach: "My God, Wia, you never told me you had redheads in your family!"

And the baby, that was you. Your parents were the first ones to fall in love, the first ones to get married, and you were the first baby to be born. That is why all through the years you have been our first child, our Berlin child. My sons were born elsewhere, Mistou's, too, and your brother was born in Rome, if I remember correctly."

Olga has enjoyed telling the story. She went deep into the past in search of happy memories. Memories shared by Claire, Wia, Rolanne, Plumette, Mistou, and Léon de Rosen. All of them agree that the best years of their lives, the most intense, were in Berlin. They were young, with a crazy desire to forget the suffering of the war and to help other people. To look for those who had disappeared, and find them, and save them: this was in keeping with the expectations they had of themselves. And it cemented their friendship. They were all, men and women alike, admirably discreet and modest about all they had done.

And now in 2008 only Olga and Plumette can still bear witness. Wia was the first to die, very early, much too early. Thirty years later it was Claire's turn, then Rolanne, Mistou, and Léon de Rosen.

In her apartment on the rue Daru, not far from the Saint Alexander Nevsky Russian Orthodox Cathedral, Olga still remembers. She takes my questions very seriously, and doesn't want to make any mistakes in her answers. Her silence, when she pauses for thought, provides an interlude for me to see those people, now gone forever, as if they had been resuscitated. My admiration for them astonishes her.

"We were lucky to have survived, and our mission to find the displaced persons was cobbled together with a great sense of urgency. We didn't know each other, we all came from very different backgrounds, but we had one thing in common: we were alive. And then Léon and Wia had so much fantastic energy, and the girls from the Red Cross were so brave, and then . . . "

A mischievous smile lights up Olga's beautiful face.

" . . . and then there was this love between your parents. A love that dazzled us, and was reflected upon us and bound us close together. It was something that made us all incredibly happy, made us want to support their good fortune, their marriage, and your birth, my Berlin child."

A new silence. Not a sound in the big empty apartment. The tea on the tray has been cold for a long time now, and we haven't touched the cakes which Olga carefully arranged on a plate two hours earlier. It's a winter afternoon, and growing dark. I get up to light the lamps, and gaze at the framed photographs of Olga and Léon de Rosen, who got married in 1948, just before the team at 96 Kurfürstendamm split up for good; there are also portraits of their children at various stages in life, and their numerous grandchildren. Group photographs, celebrations, a united family. A knot of sorrow is lodged in my throat. I think of Claire and Wia, and their short years of happiness.

Olga is still a very intuitive woman, and she seems to understand what I am feeling. Or perhaps quite simply our thoughts are going in the same direction.

"After Berlin, life was never the same. It was never easy for us, as you know."

She seems to be struggling for words.

"Your parents were so in love, yet later they came up against all those differences in their backgrounds. They really were night and day. Try to imagine them. Your father, like the sun, bursting with energy, an extrovert, always ready to throw a party; your mother, at times so dark, reluctant to go up to people, with her migraines, her never-ending migraines . . . I remember thinking, when I saw Claire and Wia at their wedding: 'To have that kind of vitality, as Wia does, then Claire with her migraines and indigestion . . . He will never be able to understand her, one day he will find fault with her for shutting herself away in a dark room for days at a time.' Yes, I remember thinking that . . . Do you want me to tell you what else I remember thinking?"

She has guessed rather than heard my murmured consent.

"You'll have to make an effort, and imagine where your Russian grandparents came from. On the day of Claire and Wia's wedding, on one side you had the French party, so elegant, and then the Russians, who were anything but. They had been through four years of war and it was particularly hard on them. They had become so poor, they didn't know how to dress or how to fit in. At least the exquisite Princess Sophie didn't. But it was typical for that era, so typical . . . I'm telling you this to help you understand your mother, who was so typically French, not at all international or cosmopolitan, and your father, who was just the opposite. But they did love each other, yes . . . In my entire life, I never saw anything like it . . . "

Olga is beginning to look tired. We have spent the afternoon together going back in time in search of Claire, Wia, and the others. She had prepared carefully for our meeting, she had sorted through her memories. Without my asking, she had resolved to be as honest and open as possible. I glance at my watch and I see it is time to leave; I rise from the sofa where I have been sitting. But Olga motions to me to sit back down.

"I'm sure you already know this, but you nearly died when you were born. If it had not been for the German doctor, you would not be sitting here now. He saved your life. A few years later he was arrested, condemned and hanged: he was a war criminal. When we found out, we were not particularly shocked. We had not yet had time to measure the full horror of the extermination of the Jews, we didn't know everything, or we weren't yet ready to know everything, I can't really recall which. In 1945, 1946, and even in May 1947, they needed us in Berlin. There were still so many people who had disappeared: we had to find them, and save them, and get them back to their families . . . "

In the cold winter night I wander somewhat aimlessly along the rue Daru, and the rue de la Neva, around the Saint Alexander Nevsky Russian Orthodox Cathedral. On her doorstep, as I was leaving, Olga held me back for a moment as if she had something else to tell me about what was then and is no more, something about forgetting. Then she shrugged her shoulders. "*Nichevo, nichevo,*" she murmured.

Anne Wiazemsky is an acclaimed French actress, author and filmmaker born in West Berlin. She has written several award winning novels: *Des filles bien élevées* (La Société des gens de lettres Grand Prix for the Novel, 1988), *Canines* (Goncourt Prize, 1993), *Hymnes à l'amour* (1996, prix RTL-Lire), and *Une poignée de gens* (The French Academy's Grand Prix, 1998). Wiazemsky was married to the director Jean-Luc Godard and she appeared in his films *La Chinoise* and *Weekend*. She lives in France.

Carmine Abate
Between Two Seas
"A moving portrayal of generational continuity."
—*Kirkus*
224 pp • $14.95 • 978-1-933372-40-2

Salwa Al Neimi
The Proof of the Honey
"Al Neimi announces the end of a taboo in the Arab world:
that of *sex!*"
—*Reuters*
144 pp • $15.00 • 978-1-933372-68-6

Alberto Angela
A Day in the Life of Ancient Rome
"Fascinating and accessible."
—*Il Giornale*
392 pp • $16.00 • 978-1-933372-71-6

Muriel Barbery
The Elegance of the Hedgehog
"Gently satirical, exceptionally winning and inevitably bittersweet."
—Michael Dirda, *The Washington Post*
336 pp • $15.00 • 978-1-933372-60-0

Gourmet Rhapsody
"In the pages of this book, Barbery shows off her finest gift: lightness."
—*La Repubblica*
176 pp • $15.00 • 978-1-933372-95-2

Stefano Benni
Margherita Dolce Vita
"A modern fable...hilarious social commentary."—*People*
240 pp • $14.95 • 978-1-933372-20-4

Timeskipper
"Benni again unveils his Italian brand of magical realism."
—*Library Journal*
400 pp • $16.95 • 978-1-933372-44-0

Romano Bilenchi
The Chill
120 pp • $15.00 • 978-1-933372-90-7

Massimo Carlotto
The Goodbye Kiss
"A masterpiece of Italian noir."
—*Globe and Mail*
160 pp • $14.95 • 978-1-933372-05-1

Death's Dark Abyss
"A remarkable study of corruption and redemption."
—*Kirkus* (starred review)
160 pp • $14.95 • 978-1-933372-18-1

The Fugitive
"[Carlotto is] the reigning king of Mediterranean noir."
—*The Boston Phoenix*
176 pp • $14.95 • 978-1-933372-25-9

(with Marco Videtta)
Poisonville
"The business world as described by Carlotto and Videtta
in *Poisonville* is frightening as hell."
—*La Repubblica*
224 pp • $15.00 • 978-1-933372-91-4

Francisco Coloane
Tierra del Fuego
"Coloane is the Jack London of our times."—Alvaro Mutis
192 pp • $14.95 • 978-1-933372-63-1

Giancarlo De Cataldo
The Father and the Foreigner
"A slim but touching noir novel from one of Italy's best writers
in the genre."—*Quaderni Noir*
144 pp • $15.00 • 978-1-933372-72-3

Shashi Deshpande
The Dark Holds No Terrors
"[Deshpande is] an extremely talented storyteller."—*Hindustan Times*
272 pp • $15.00 • 978-1-933372-67-9

Helmut Dubiel
Deep In the Brain: Living with Parkinson's Disease
"A book that begs reflection."—*Die Zeit*
144 pp • $15.00 • 978-1-933372-70-9

Steve Erickson
Zeroville
"A funny, disturbing, daring and demanding novel—Erickson's best."
—*The New York Times Book Review*
352 pp • $14.95 • 978-1-933372-39-6

Elena Ferrante
The Days of Abandonment
"The raging, torrential voice of [this] author is something rare."
—*The New York Times*
192 pp • $14.95 • 978-1-933372-00-6

Troubling Love
"Ferrante's polished language belies the rawness of her imagery."
—*The New Yorker*
144 pp • $14.95 • 978-1-933372-16-7

The Lost Daughter
"So refined, almost translucent."—*The Boston Globe*
144 pp • $14.95 • 978-1-933372-42-6

Jane Gardam
Old Filth
"Old Filth belongs in the Dickensian pantheon of memorable characters."
—*The New York Times Book Review*
304 pp • $14.95 • 978-1-933372-13-6

The Queen of the Tambourine
"A truly superb and moving novel."—*The Boston Globe*
272 pp • $14.95 • 978-1-933372-36-5

The People on Privilege Hill
"Engrossing stories of hilarity and heartbreak."—*Seattle Times*
208 pp • $15.95 • 978-1-933372-56-3

The Man in the Wooden Hat
"Here is a writer who delivers the world we live in…with memorable and moving skill."—*The Boston Globe*
240 pp • $15.00 • 978-1-933372-89-1

Alicia Giménez-Bartlett
Dog Day
"Delicado and Garzón prove to be one of the more engaging sleuth teams to debut in a long time."—*The Washington Post*
320 pp • $14.95 • 978-1-933372-14-3

Prime Time Suspect
"A gripping police procedural."—*The Washington Post*
320 pp • $14.95 • 978-1-933372-31-0

Death Rites
"Petra is developing into a good cop, and her earnest efforts to assert her authority…are worth cheering."—*The New York Times*
304 pp • $16.95 • 978-1-933372-54-9

Katharina Hacker
The Have-Nots
"Hacker's prose soars."—*Publishers Weekly*
352 pp • $14.95 • 978-1-933372-41-9

Patrick Hamilton
Hangover Square
"Patrick Hamilton's novels are dark tunnels of misery, loneliness, deceit, and sexual obsession."—*New York Review of Books*
336 pp • $14.95 • 978-1-933372-06-

James Hamilton-Paterson
Cooking with Fernet Branca
"Irresistible!"—*The Washington Post*
288 pp • $14.95 • 978-1-933372-01-3

Amazing Disgrace
"It's loads of fun, light and dazzling as a peacock feather."
—*New York Magazine*
352 pp • $14.95 • 978-1-933372-19-8

Rancid Pansies
"Campy comic saga about hack writer and self-styled 'culinary genius' Gerald Samper."—*Seattle Times*
288 pp • $15.95 • 978-1-933372-62-4

Seven-Tenths: The Sea and Its Thresholds
"The kind of book that, were he alive now, Shelley might have written."
—*Charles Spawson*
416 pp • $16.00 • 978-1-933372-69-3

Alfred Hayes
The Girl on the Via Flaminia
"Immensely readable."—*The New York Times*
164 pp • $14.95 • 978-1-933372-24-2

Jean-Claude Izzo
Total Chaos
"Izzo's Marseilles is ravishing."—*Globe and Mail*
256 pp • $14.95 • 978-1-933372-04-4

Chourmo
"A bitter, sad and tender salute to a place equally impossible to love
or leave."—*Kirkus* (starred review)
256 pp • $14.95 • 978-1-933372-17-4

Solea
"[Izzo is] a talented writer who draws from the deep, dark well of noir."
—*The Washington Post*
208 pp • $14.95 • 978-1-933372-30-3

The Lost Sailors
"Izzo digs deep into what makes men weep."—*Time Out New York*
272 pp • $14.95 • 978-1-933372-35-8

A Sun for the Dying
"Beautiful, like a black sun, tragic and desperate."—*Le Point*
224 pp • $15.00 • 978-1-933372-59-4

Gail Jones
Sorry
"Jones's gift for conjuring place and mood rarely falters."
—*Times Literary Supplement*
240 pp • $15.95 • 978-1-933372-55-6

Matthew F. Jones
Boot Tracks
"A gritty action tale."—*The Philadelphia Inquirer*
208 pp • $14.95 • 978-1-933372-11-2

Ioanna Karystiani
The Jasmine Isle
"A modern Greek tragedy about love foredoomed and family life."
—*Kirkus*
288 pp • $14.95 • 978-1-933372-10-5

Swell
"Karystiani movingly pays homage to the sea and those who live from it."
—*La Repubblica*
256 pp • $15.00 • 978-1-933372-98-3

Gene Kerrigan
The Midnight Choir
"The lethal precision of his closing punches leave quite a lasting mark."
—*Entertainment Weekly*
368 pp • $14.95 • 978-1-933372-26-6

Little Criminals
"A great story...relentless and brilliant."—*Roddy Doyle*
352 pp • $16.95 • 978-1-933372-43-3

Peter Kocan
Fresh Fields
"A stark, harrowing, yet deeply courageous work of immense power and
magnitude."—*Quadrant*
304 pp • $14.95 • 978-1-933372-29-7

The Treatment and the Cure
"Kocan tells this story with grace and humor."—*Publishers Weekly*
256 pp • $15.95 • 978-1-933372-45-7

Helmut Krausser
Eros
"Helmut Krausser has succeeded in writing a great German epochal novel."—*Focus*
352 pp • $16.95 • 978-1-933372-58-7

Amara Lakhous
Clash of Civilizations Over an Elevator in Piazza Vittorio
"Do we have an Italian Camus on our hands? Just possibly."
—*The Philadelphia Inquirer*
144 pp • $14.95 • 978-1-933372-61-7

Lia Levi
The Jewish Husband
"An exemplary tale of small lives engulfed in the vortex of history."
—*Il Messaggero*
224 pp • $15.00 • 978-1-933372-93-8

Carlo Lucarelli
Carte Blanche
"Lucarelli proves that the dark and sinister are better evoked when one opts for unadulterated grit and grime."—*The San Diego Union-Tribune*
128 pp • $14.95 • 978-1-933372-15-0

The Damned Season
"De Luca…is a man both pursuing and pursued. And that makes him one of the more interesting figures in crime fiction."
—*The Philadelphia Inquirer*
128 pp • $14.95 • 978-1-933372-27-3

Via delle Oche
"Delivers a resolution true to the series' moral relativism."—*Publishers Weekly*
160 pp • $14.95 • 978-1-933372-53-2

Edna Mazya
Love Burns
"Combines the suspense of a murder mystery with
the absurdity of a Woody Allen movie."—*Kirkus*
224 pp • $14.95 • 978-1-933372-08-2

Sélim Nassib
I Loved You for Your Voice
"Nassib spins a rhapsodic narrative out of the indissoluble
connection between two creative souls."—*Kirkus*
272 pp • $14.95 • 978-1-933372-07-5

The Palestinian Lover
"A delicate, passionate novel in which history and life
are inextricably entwined."
—*RAI Books*
192 pp • $14.95 • 978-1-933372-23-5

Amélie Nothomb
Tokyo Fiancée
"Intimate and honest…depicts perfectly a nontraditional romance."
—*Publishers Weekly*
160 pp • $15.00 • 978-1-933372-64-8

Valeria Parrella
For Grace Received
"A voice that is new, original, and decidedly unique."—*Rolling Stone* (Italy)
144 pp • $15.00 • 978-1-933372-94-5

Alessandro Piperno
The Worst Intentions
"A coruscating mixture of satire, family epic, Proustian meditation, and erotomaniacal farce."—*The New Yorker*
320 pp • $14.95 • 978-1-933372-33-4

Boualem Sansal
The German Mujahid
"Terror, doubt, revolt, guilt, and despair—a surprising range of emotions is admirably and convincingly depicted in this incredible novel."
—*L'Express* (France)
240 pp • $15.00 • 978-1-933372-92-1

Eric-Emmanuel Schmitt
The Most Beautiful Book in the World
"Eight novellas, parables on the idea of a future, filled with redeeming optimism."—*Lire Magazine*
192 pp • $15.00 • 978-1-933372-74-7

Domenico Starnone
First Execution
"Starnone's books are small theatres of action, both physical and psychological."—*L'Espresso* (Italy)
176 pp • $15.00 • 978-1-933372-66-2

Joel Stone
The Jerusalem File
"Joel Stone is a major new talent."—*Cleveland Plain Dealer*
160 pp • $15.00 • 978-1-933372-65-5

Benjamin Tammuz
Minotaur
"A novel about the expectations and compromises that humans create for themselves."—*The New York Times*
192 pp • $14.95 • 978-1-933372-02-0

Chad Taylor
Departure Lounge
"There's so much pleasure and bafflement to be derived from this thriller."
—*The Chicago Tribune*
176 pp • $14.95 • 978-1-933372-09-9

Roma Tearne
Mosquito
"Vividly rendered...Wholly satisfying."—*Kirkus*
304 pp • $16.95 • 978-1-933372-57-0

Bone China
"Tearne deftly reveals the corrosive effects of civil strife on private lives and the redemptiveness of art."—*The Guardian*
400 pp • $16.00 • 978-1-933372-75-4

Christa Wolf
One Day a Year: 1960-2000
"Remarkable!"—*The New Yorker*
640 pp • $16.95 • 978-1-933372-22-8